# BENEATH THE BURNING HILLS

## STEFAN TAYLOR

*To Mum and Dad.*

# AUTHOR'S NOTE

*Beneath the Burning Hills* is a sequel to my previous releases, *Beyond the Boundary Fence* and *Until the Storm Passes.*

While both of those stories can be read separately, and independently of each other, this story follows on from the events of those two books.

I felt the characters had more of their story to tell, and more to explore.

Also, eagle-eyed readers may have noted the familiar name of the estate that Lilly and Jordan were heading to at the end of *Until the Storm Passes.*

*Beneath the Burning Hills* takes place two years after the events of *Beyond the Boundary Fence,* and two months after the events of *Until the Storm Passes.*

The man screamed.

The creature smiled.

Its talons tore into flesh, and his howls rang through the expansive cave where he hung, vines digging into his wrists. Blood fountained from the wide laceration to his stomach, splashing on the cave's walls to pool upon the floor.

Life faded.

His eyes told the story of the weeks of pain endured. When the end came, those tortured eyes blinked shut as if he was falling into blissful sleep.

The creature's smile widened. Not at the human's passing. Its smile was for what it had ripped from the man's grotesquely swollen stomach.

A tangle of grey slugs slid from the dangling corpse, plopping to the moist earth below.

The young are born, the creature thought joyously.

Gathering the tangled, glistening mass, it brought them to a shallow pool in the centre of the cavern, lowering them into the inky water. Its pale eyes softened as it gazed upon them. Laying close to the water's edge, its smile now threatened to split its face. A contented, almost gleeful hiss escaped its throat.

Its screams were too loud; you should have killed it first! The words were suddenly pushed into the creature's mind, and its eyes darted to the dark above.

The creature relaxed beneath the pale eyes that blinked open in the gloom. Its kin had arrived.

*You missed the birthing,* it replied in its mind to the other, thinking of the two cycles of the four seasons that had passed since the young two-legs had burned their cave, leaving their entire pack—their newborns and leader—nothing but ash.

The creature's breath was a puff of mist in the damp air. Reaching out again with its mind, thoughts passed effortlessly between the two.

*Anyway, I thought you enjoyed it's suffering?* It asked. The other descended to join it.

*Its screams may be heard by other two-legs. They may bring fire!'* the other thought.

*Fear not, the earth above us swallows the screams.*

The other's eyes narrowed to razor-thin slits. *We are all that remain. If any harm comes to the young, it will be our end!*

Now the memories of the two-leg's attack on their subterranean home flooded their thoughts. The mist of their breathing spilled faster into the air, bodies trembling as the memories of smoke and flames danced once again in their collective minds.

*When the young are grown, the two-legs will pay! We shall take back the world of men.*

But its fellow shook its great head and slunk back into shadow, serpent tail swishing through the mud of the cave floor as it went.

The creature slumped with a defeated sigh by the pool. Its head resting on bony arms as it thought of the years they'd worked to build their numbers, to ready themselves to take back the world above. A world infested with two-legs.

But their plan had fallen to ruin.

Their leader was dead, their pack almost gone. *Extinction...* The creature banished the thought. It was going to be a long and painful path to rebuilding. A groan slipped free as it pushed the thoughts aside before moving toward the human figure hanging lifeless from the vines. This one had been strong of body, but weak of mind, making it easy to trap.

It cut the vines and the human crumpled to the cave floor. Casually it tore an arm free, biting eagerly into pulpy flesh. The two-legs were a plague on the land, true; but they made a tasty meal. It chomped down on the limb before opening its mind to call back its kin to share in the feast.

It stilled. The meal suddenly forgotten.

Tilting its head to the roof of the cave, it opened its senses to the world above. A gentle spark of energy flickered like a lamp bobbing on the surface of a great ocean by night. A soft glow in the vast mental void where, for so long, there had been only darkness.

Its kin scurried from the shadows. *Did you sense that?*

The creature's eyes squeezed shut as it probed the distant light. *A mind! So strong! So... strange.* Both slithered toward the exit of the cave. Then as it probed the light further, it frowned with confusion. *That mind I... I think it is... a... a two-leg!*

*Impossible,* its kin scoffed. *Never has a human been able to enter the void let alone discover it!*

*Feel how scattered the thoughts are? That is a human mind!* The creature's breath steamed in the air. *We need to wake the Monarch.*

The mention of the great elder caused the other to cower. *But the Monarch must not be awakened until the day of our rising. We must rebuild our numbers to open the gate, remember? Or we won't have enough power! He will be furious!*

'*But a mind... a human mind, no less, that burns like that and illuminates the void? Surely, the Monarch must be told?*

Silence fell between them. Tails swishing through the mud below.

The other's eyes went wide. *Send the Seeker first,* it suggested. *We should ensure we know what we are dealing with first.*

The creature nodded. Looking to the shadows of the cave's roof, it called the Seeker.

A moment later something serpentine slithered from above and hurried toward it. Although born of the same ilk as its masters, it was a basic, thoughtless thing in comparison. Yet it was linked to them by the same telepathic abilities.

The creature's eyes locked on the Seeker, and the thing's head tilted as if listening. The spark in the void throbbed brighter in their minds.

*Seek the being that is the source of that light. Do not be seen!*

The Seeker slithered away, swallowed by the darkness as it journeyed to the world above.

Its kin finally joined the creature by their young and together, they opened their minds to the great mental void. The light faded like the sun dipping below the horizon.

They concentrated their thoughts, sending out their simple message: *Join us, join us… join us…*

The light pulsed brighter.

J uggling a collection of crayons in her elfin hand, Lilly Jenkins wiped a thin sheen of sweat from her brow, eyes falling to her work. The driveway was coated in swirling rainbow patterns and dancing shapes, all the way up to the expansive, open garage attached to her new home. The garage that looked so much like a cave.

She grinned at her work. The driveway had been too bland; much like the new suburb she and her sister had found themselves in. Squinting against the sun, she gazed up and down the wide street. Never in her short life of seven years, had she seen such a dull collection of houses than the ones making up the Golden Pastures Estate.

Every house was built in the same style. Everyone seemed to drive the same car. Everything looked the same, making it difficult to tell one house from another.

Sighing wistfully, she returned to shading in a new patch of the driveway. Her smile quickly returned as she beheld her creation. Uncle Henry would love this!

After all, he was always excited to see her new pictures; and often stuck them on the fridge, or by his workbench in the shed.

*He'll love his new driveway.*

A sudden, rough tap on her shoulder caused her to spin about. A shock of bright pink hair came into focus. Below that shock of pink was the grim face of her sister, Jordan.

Nine years older than Lilly, and about nine times taller too; Jordan stood with hands on her hips. Dressed in her black training shorts and singlet, her head shaved down one side, at first sight, many neighbours had initially assumed Jordan was Lilly's older brother.

This was a common mistake her sister was not quick to forgive. Jordan breathed heavily, flicked sweat from her eyes. Squatting beside Lilly, she snatched one of the crayons from her. "Did Uncle Henry say you could ruin his driveway?"

Deaf since she was a toddler; Lilly didn't hear the words, although she could read lips as clear as reading words on a page. Lilly had also excelled in learning sign language. Afterall, what choice did she have?

"Well?" Jordan pressed, brandishing the crayon in Lilly's face.

Shaking her head, Lilly looked away. It was best not to challenge Jordan when she was in one of these dark moods. They were more common now since that terror they'd faced in Barnsford. Jordan had become horribly strict on Lilly. Everything had changed when they'd stopped in that awful town.

Desperately, Lilly tried to block the thoughts of that place, and that... *thing* that had taken their brother from them. Yet the harder she tried to ignore the memories of that terrible place; the harder they forced their way into her mind.

Squeezing her eyes shut, she tried to drive the memories away. Only a couple of months had passed since their ordeal, and the memories were still very fresh.

Another agitated tap on her shoulder.

Lilly opened her eyes, and Jordan's sweaty face came back into focus.

'What's wrong?' Jordan signed the question this time.

Lilly shook her head, not wanting to bring up the town or their brother, Owen.

She hoped Owen would get better soon. Tears welled in Lilly's eyes, and Jordan slapped the crayon back into her hand with a dismissive shake of her head.

'Ask first,' Jordan signed, and moved back into the garage where a large boxing bag dangled from one of the roof beams.

Slipping on a pair of faded boxing gloves, Jordan stalked around the bag throwing lightning-fast kicks and punches.

The garage's ceiling shook with every strike. Lilly couldn't hear the impact of the hits, but she could feel the anger behind them.

It seemed to Lilly that Jordan's only real passion in life was martial arts, and she practised every morning and every night without fail. If her sister wasn't practising at home, she was training at the small kickboxing gym in the shopping plaza.

Now that the holidays had commenced, neither had started at their new schools apart from a few days of orientation. So, all her sister did was practise, practise, and practise some more.

It was clear that what they experienced in Barnsford had deeply changed Jordan. She'd always been moody, but that town had made her grim, angry and… frightened?

Lilly wiped the beginnings of tears away. It was going to be ok now. They were starting a new life. But Owen's face flashed in her mind again. He was more than her brother. He was father to them both and had looked after them so lovingly since the passing of their parents. More than that, he had been her best friend.

*I had another friend as well.*

She winced as her stomach knotted at the memory of her special friend. She'd named it the Happy One because that was how it had always made her feel. The Happy One had been the joined spirits of her parents, and they had been watching over her, helping where they could. But she'd lost them in the town of Barnsford as well.

Lilly sniffed back the tears that threatened to overwhelm her. *That place took everything.*

A lashing of loneliness fell upon her. Closing her eyes, she opened herself to the void in her mind where once the Happy One would speak with her. The void spread on forever. A great plain of darkness, empty now. It was as if the Happy One had never even existed there at all.

A choked sigh escaped her, and she pushed to her feet and dusted off her glittering, summer dress. The urge to draw had deserted her, along with the joy it brought. Gathering the many crayons scattered across the driveway, she moved toward the house when there was a flash in the void!

The crayons tumbled from her hands, and she spun to face the far end of the street.

While the land had been cleared to construct more homes, none had ever been built. Instead, dry and patchy earth was scattered with long, swaying grass in the abandoned area.

Beyond the grass, a tall and rusty fence stood. Jordan had said it marked the boundary of the estate. Their new house was the last before the empty plots.

Trotting down the driveway, Lilly peered at the bushland beyond. Somewhere, in the vast mental void, she could've sworn she'd felt a spark of energy, and she was just as sure it had emanated from that direction. For a moment, she stood staring toward the bush.

Was something out there? Something that had the same ability to access the void that she did? Bouncing up and down on her tiptoes, she closed her eyes and stretched her mind across the mental plane.

*Hello?*

There! A spark of energy!

Yet as quickly as it came, it was gone. The feeling was like water slipping through her fingers. Something was there, and it had sensed her! Dashing back to the garage where Jordan was pumping out a set of sit-ups on the rough, concrete floor, she cautiously tapped her sister's shoulder.

Dark eyes shot up, locking on to hers. Jordan hopped to her feet. 'What?' she signed.

'Can I play in the grass?' Lilly signed back excitedly.

Her sister glanced at the empty plots and shook her head.

'I won't go far.' Lilly signed again.

'No, stay where I can see you.' Jordan signed back.

'I just want to look around.' Lilly gave her sister pleading eyes.

Jordan grabbed Lilly's shoulders, the iron grip crushing her slender arms. "Did you sense something?" Jordan demanded; not bothering to sign.

Lilly shook her head quickly.

Jordan eyed her for a moment before releasing her. "When Uncle Henry gets home, maybe he'll take you over to the playground."

'Could *you* take me?' Lilly signed.

"No," Jordan said simply, and turned back to the punching bag.

Lilly stamped her foot in frustration while pulling at her sister's arm.

Jordan swung to glower down at her.

Lilly knew she was poking the Lion, but she didn't care. 'You never let me do anything! Why can't we go to the park, or the shops?' Lilly signed. 'Why won't you play with me anymore?'

Lilly felt the bright summer day darken as her sister gazed coldly down on her. She suddenly regretted pushing the point with Jordan.

"You know why," her sister said.

Lilly gulped in fear but Jordan's eyes softened. Nodding to the entrance of the house, she gently guided Lilly away. "Go and play on your Tablet or something. I need to practise."

Not needing to be told twice, Lilly gathered her crayons from the driveway and, feeling her sister's eyes burning into her back, escaped inside.

Plodding down the wide hall to her bedroom and picking her way over the mess of drawings littering the floor, Lilly climbed on her bed and tugged the blinds open. Brilliant sunlight flooded the room.

The empty plots and bush came into view over the low side-fence of their property.

Again, she closed her eyes and opened her thoughts. She could sense something out in that wilderness, just on the edge of her mind.

What was it? Energy? A thought? Both? Some words drifted to her. Weak like the suggestion of a breeze in the air.

Then a distant thought came to her. Muffled, as if layers of earth supressed it. But for just a second the thought was clear.

*Join us, Join us…*

2

SMACK!

The punch came from nowhere. One second, he was sitting on a bench, looking out on the school's oval, the next moment, he was lying flat on the grass, staring up at the puffy clouds drifting high above.

Brody Webb struggled onto his side, shaking his head to stop it spinning. A sharp kick stabbed his back causing him to squeal in pain.

"Get up!" a deep, crackling voice barked.

Another kick. Harder this time. Brody clutched his back helplessly.

"I said get up, you little shit!"

Rolling over, he looked up to see the blustering, tomato-red face of Mason Williams. A crowd gathered. Some students had their phones out, already recording.

Brody struggled to his feet. *Better make a show of it, at least.*

This was his third high school in two years. He thought he'd be used to the endless cycle of bullying, but he'd been thinking that since he was a kid. Out of all the kids who pushed him as he walked the school halls, or spat in his food at lunch, Mason was the worst by far.

Brody was his walking punching bag. Not a single week went by where Mason didn't chase him down and smash his head into a locker or bash him until he was hardly able to stand.

Now they stood before each other like David and Goliath. Only Brody had no slingshot up his sleeve to defeat this monster.

Stretching himself to his full height, still clutching his back, Brody found himself about level with Mason's chest. "Just leave me alone! I've never done anything to you—"

"You're a piece of shit murderer!" Mason yelled, punching Brody hard in the face with a short jab.

Brody tumbled back over the bench, crashing on his already screaming spine.

Mason let rip a series of brutal kicks square in his stomach. Brody gagged, forcing the vomit back down. The crowd hooted and laughed cruelly at the scene. He watched Mason raise his fists in the air and smile at them.

Looking back up to the puffy clouds above, Brody allowed himself a flicker of fantasy. He imagined himself soaring through those clouds. Free and fearless. "Get up, murderer!"

There it was again. Mason said it for all to hear. The reason his torment had gotten worse at every school since leaving Golden Pastures.

Dropping his head, he breathed deeply, trying to supress the stirring memories of two years ago. He'd lost two of the best—no— the *only* friends he'd ever had. He couldn't tell the truth about what had happened. Who would believe it anyway? Hadn't Old Pete said exactly that? The image of his elderly friend appeared before his eyes – glowing white beard and tattered clothes, bushy eyebrows framing sparkling eyes. Pete's warning still rung through the boy's mind: *"Stay out of the bush!"*

They should have listened, but they couldn't have left Todd out there alone with those things.

When the media got hold of the story, it had seemed straight forward enough to everyone. Three children went looking for their missing friend. One fell down an old mine shaft, got lost below. The remaining two children, also lost and disorientated, lit a fire to attract the attention of the rescuers. The fire spread, and sadly the bodies of their two friends had never been found.

Some people had suggested that their story just didn't add up. Which was true in a sense. Afterall, they had made it up to cover the truth of what lurked in the bushland. But there were those who had theorised that he and Zoe had lit the fires to cover up evidence of the murder of their friends.

These rumours grew rampant online. Videos started to appear accusing them of killing Mike and Todd. Of course, there was no proof of this. But when did the truth get in the way of a good conspiracy theory?

He looked around at the kids gathered to watch his demise. Same as all those other kids from all the other schools when they had discovered he was Brody Webb from the mysterious Golden Pastures disappearances. They'd made his life an endless parade of assaults and bullying. Yet somehow, he managed to bear it. What other choice did he have?

Mason yanked Brody to his feet, and he was suddenly back in the present.

"I should just beat you to death right here," Mason seethed, shoving Brody back. "Think anyone would stop me? Do you think anyone cares?"

Brody took a steadying breath. If he'd learned anything from his years of dealing with bullies, it was better to go down swinging than to run.

Dropping his shoulder, he rammed Mason with every ounce of strength he could muster. The thug stumbled, glared down at him in shock. Clearly, Mason hadn't expected any resistance.

"I didn't kill them! They were my friends!" Brody launched himself at Mason, threw a volley of wild punches.

Mason laughed and simply blocked them with his bulky arms. Rough hands took hold of Brody, dragging him to the ground. Seemed three of Mason's buddies had decided to join in the festivities.

Pinning him on his back, Mason savaged Brody with kick after kick, as he lay helpless.

"That's it, hold him there!" the bully screeched, spittle dribbling from his grinning mouth. "Everyone will get a go at bashing him! This is going to be sweet!"

The crowd hooted and cheered.

Brody struggled, crying out as the harsh kicks rained down. Mason dropped down on top of him. Sweat dripped from the bully's flushed face on to Brody's. "I'm going to make sure this happens every day," he hissed. "If you ever snitch on me… I'll fucking kill you."

He brought his fist down savagely on the side of Brody's head. The world spun. Through fuzzy vision, he saw Mason raise his fist for another blow.

"Teacher!" a voice yelled.

The crowd scattered, as did his attackers.

Staggering up off the ground and lurching to the bench, spitting clumps of blood and bile, Brody snatched up his bag and pushed through the dispersing students, and headed for the fence line.

"What the bloody hell is going on here?" The gruff voice of a male teacher yelled.

Brody hobbled across the oval toward the bike sheds, spitting up more blood as he went. Dashing behind the sheds, he threw his bag over the chain link fence, clambered over, grimacing as he dropped to the other side.

Fleeing through the eerily silent suburban streets, his tears fell.

# 4

"Is everything all right Zoe?" a gentle voice murmured. They sat on two low sofas, strategically positioned to face toward the sprawling bushland across the road.

Drawing her weary eyes from the distant bushland, Zoe plastered her polite, private schoolgirl smile across her face as she spoke. "Yes, thank you, Doctor Vasakas. I'm just a bit tired."

She was getting used to putting on this front of control. Even surprising herself at how convincing she could be.

"Please, Zoe, call me Tanya. You know I hate formalities," the doctor replied in that husky, singsong voice of hers. The doctor pronounced her own name 'Tar-ni-ya' and it drove Zoe mad.

Shifting in her seat to hide her growing annoyance, Zoe stifled a yawn. God, she hated these sessions with Tar-ni-ya. But her parents insisted she saw the doctor at least once every couple of weeks. Said it was good for her to have someone to talk with; especially after everything she'd been through.

It never seemed to cross their minds that perhaps she'd have liked to talk with them instead, but they were too busy. Always, so very busy.

"Zoe? Are you all right?"

"Huh? I mean… Sorry what?" Had the doctor been talking that whole time?

"I asked if you've still been experiencing the bad dreams?"

Zoe offered a dismissive shrug.

"So, you're sleeping well? The medicine is working?"

She nodded, reapplying her fake smile.

"Your mother sent me your school report." The doctor picked up her tablet from the table between them. "It's outstanding, Zoe. Really great."

"Thank you, Doct… Tanya."

"How's the communication between you and your mother going?"

Zoe shook her head.

The doctor nodded, tapping a few notes into her tablet. After a rather awkward amount of time, she placed the tablet aside. "Your school says you're a model student. You always complete assignments on time, if not weeks early. You're acing every subject except…" She looked over at her tablet and frowned. "Outdoor education."

Zoe sniffed; she'd seen more than enough of the outdoors.

The doctor continued. "They're concerned you're withdrawing from all the social activities. Do you have any friends at boarding school?"

Again, Zoe shrugged. How was she supposed to answer that?

"What about outside school?" the doctor asked.

"It's kind of hard to have friends outside of school when you live at school."

Her challenging tone was not lost on the doctor, "Well… yes…" She cleared her throat. "But I mean, friends near home?"

Zoe's eyes snapped to the bushland then looked quickly away. "I used to."

The doctor smoothed her dress. Cleared her throat. "Apart from the friends who… passed."

That simple question brought the horrors of two years ago flooding back. The terror as the creatures pursued them. The sensation of the rank mud in her hands as she dragged herself through the caves and away from the raging fire. The flames that blistered her skin and burned her flowing curls away.

Her heart raced. Sweat built on the back of her neck. "No," she replied as calmly as she could.

Curling her lips, the doctor reached for her prescription pad. "I'm going to prescribe another round of Fluoxetine," she said, scribbling on the pad. "Enjoy your school holidays. Remember, you can email me any time you need." Tearing the prescription from the pad, she waved it at Zoe. The fake smile plastered across the doctor's face reminded

Zoe of an airline hostess on a travel poster.

Zoe returned her own fake smile.

"Thank you, Tar-ni-ya."

Scrunching up the prescription, Zoe flicked it into the bin outside the doctor's office. Hurrying across the road to the bus stop, she glared up at the hilly bushland as she approached. It seemed to stare back in challenge.

Zoe scrapped the idea of taking the bus, and started walking in the direction of the estate. She wanted to be as far away from the bush and the stupid doctor's office as possible, but she also wanted some time to just calm her thoughts. Being this close to the bush was raising her heart rate at a frightening pace. The panic was going to hit her if she didn't get the hell out of here. And quickly.

*You're being ridiculous! There's nothing watching you!*

Still, despite the bright sunshine above, she shivered.

5

Her feet pounded the familiar streets of Golden Pastures, and Zoe found herself grinning contentedly. The holidays were officially on, and she finally had some time away from school. But as thoughts of her old friends came to her, the grin faded. It wasn't the same without them.

Sure, she was on speaking terms with a few girls at school but none she would've considered friends, and certainly none that would want to catch up over the holidays. A despondent sigh escaped her, and the smile fell away.

She paused at a familiar street. Brody's street.

They'd kept their promise to keep in contact after everything had died down. But time eroded that promise, and gradually they'd faded out of each other's lives. Part of her knew that would happen, regardless of what they'd said.

Another memory pushed its way in. The two of them standing at the front of her house, Brody's earnest eyes looking up into hers, wringing his hands as he stutteringly asked her if she wanted to go out with him.

A delighted giggle brought on by the memory escaped her. She would've said yes but… there had been someone else then.

Todd.

A cloud passing in front of the sun cast a shadow as dark as the memory of him hanging helplessly in the cave. The image of the behemoth ripping him open, savaged her. Heart pumping against her ribs, cold sweat forming on her neck and back; she felt the panic coming. *That isn't how he'd want you to remember him.*

Zoe steered her thoughts to a brighter place. All of them – Todd, Mike, Brody, and her. All together. Drinking, laughing and just… being.

"Hey, baby!" An obnoxious voice broke her melancholic reflections. Startled, she whipped about to see three boys, roughly her age, on the opposite side of the road. All were dressed in lose-fitting shorts and singlets.

One sat astride a mountain bike, his feet struggling to reach the ground. Their eyes leered over her, fixing on her chest and legs.

"My friend here thinks you're hot," the boy on the bike announced. "You want his number?" They chuckled to each other.

She didn't even bother replying, just headed down the street.

"Bitch," she heard the obnoxious voice mutter as she turned. Quickening her steps, she heard the whiz of the bike gaining on her.

He caught up, peddling around her in a slow circle, a sly grin twisting across his skeleton-thin face. "Why don't you come and hang out?" He raised an eyebrow at his friends. "We could have a little party, what do you think?"

Stepping off the street, she hurried toward a pathway that ran behind the houses.

He sped up beside her, hand whipping out to clutch her arm. "Hey! I don't like being ignored," he said, wicked eyes fixing on hers.

"Don't touch me!" she growled, tearing her arm from his grip.

"Do I make you nervous, baby? I promise I'll be gentle if it's your first time." His voice oozed through wet lips.

Hands fisted at her sides; she locked her eyes on his. "Touch me again, and I'll bash your ugly skull in!"

He scoffed, folding his arms as he did. "Is that so, little girl?"

"I've faced things way worse than you, *little boy*. And none of them are around to talk about it. So go on, try me." Her jaw clenched; she almost hoped he would.

Uncertainty, drifted across his eyes. He wheeled the bike back a few paces. It was clear he hadn't expected this. She snapped her fist back, pretending she was about to strike.

He flinched, but quickly steadied himself.

"Go on," she said darkly. "Touch me again. See what happens."

He swallowed, eyes darting to his friends. But then he burst into clearly forced laughter. "I was… I'm just… just playing around. Can't you take a joke?" He rode quickly away. All cast nervous glances as they retreated. The one on the bike blew her a kiss, but only when he was at a safe distance.

Stamping down the path, barely paying attention to where she was heading, Zoe tried to smother the anger within her. Her face was flushed with heat. If she saw that prick again, she'd make sure he got what was coming to him. Thinking he could lay a hand on her like that and get away with it—

She jerked to a halt. Her throat suddenly dry as she realised where she was.

The empty plots were at the far end of the street before her. It was like it had appeared to say, 'Welcome home, Zoe.'

Her panic built. *I gotta get out of here.*

Movement caught her eye. Something was struggling through the long grass of the plots. A pang of dread smacked into her gut when she saw what it was.

A little girl! Picking her way toward the boundary fence! Had the child heard the call of the things in the bush? No, that wasn't possible. They were all dead… Weren't they?

Zoe sprinted toward the child. Pulling up just below the streetlamp, she called out. The child stood at the rusted fence, tiny hands clasping the wire.

"Hey! You shouldn't be down here!" Zoe called. But the child continued staring into the shadowy bushland. "Hey!" Zoe yelled again, her voice echoing around the clearing. Still, the child didn't move. Her skin rose in goose bumps. The creatures! Their calls! The psychic words that froze the victim to the spot!

*They're back!*

Her own terror forgotten, she rushed across the brittle earth to the girl, spun the child around and gripped her by the arms.

The child squealed in shock, pulling her hands in protectively.

"Are you all right?" Zoe cried into the child's face.

The little girl stared wide-eyed at her in fright. Zoe realised the child wasn't being controlled and a wave of relief washed over her.

There were no creatures out there. Of course there weren't. She'd just terrified this poor kid for nothing. Dropping her hands, she forced a smile for the rightfully frightened child. "Oh, God. I'm so sorry. I thought…"

The girl watched her lips intently.

"Listen, you shouldn't play down here. It isn't safe."

The child relaxed a bit, looking Zoe up and down.

"I'm Zoe, what's your name?"

The child gripped her bright dress and looked away nervously.

*You've scared the kid half to death.* As a last resort, Zoe unleashed her private-school smile. It hadn't failed yet. "I'm so sorry, I really didn't mean to frighten you. Do you live nearby?"

The child returned a shy smile, then stood up straight, touched her throat and shook her head.

"I don't understand. Are you lost? Where are your—"

"Oi!"

The voice crashed through the air like a clap of thunder. Zoe wheeled around and immediately slunk back when she saw the speaker.

The girl striding across the empty plots toward them was a knot of angry muscle. Her every movement seemed dangerous. The shock of pink hair crowning her head was matted with sweat.

Furiously, the girl motioned the child to join her. The kid scurried to obey. Folding her arms, this newcomer fixed Zoe with a look that could shatter stone. "You hassling my sister?" she growled, stepping in front of her protectively.

Zoe glanced between the two. Sisters?

The pink haired girl bent to eye the child. "You snuck out, didn't you?" she said slowly.

The child looked to her feet; shame written in her eyes.

The older girl grabbed her arm roughly. "Get inside! Now!"

Zoe frowned as the pink haired girl gestured with her hands as she spoke. *The kid is deaf!*

Struggling through the long grass, the kid hurried toward one of the large, houses on the edge of the empty plots. The sister powered toward her, and Zoe found herself backing up into the fence, cringing at the feel of the shadowed bushland behind her. *Talk about a rock and a hard place.*

The girl cracked her neck, glaring down at Zoe with menace. "And you are?"

"Z-Z-Zoe."

"Well, Z-Z-Zoe, you stay away from her, understand?"

"I was just… it's not safe down here—"

"What do you mean?" the girl demanded.

"The bush. It's easy to get lost in there…happens all the time to people."

A sneer crept across the pink-haired girl's face. "You're right," she said. "It's not safe down here. Better get home, rich girl."

Not needing to be told twice, Zoe stepped cautiously around the girl and hastened toward the road. As she made her way past the house, she saw the little girl smile sadly at her from a front window.

It seemed the monsters in the bush had been replaced by this pink-haired beast.

6

rody felt his mother's eyes on him as he stacked the dishwasher. Smiling quickly over his shoulder at her, she flashed a thoughtful smile back. With her arms folded, she wore a soft expression. He knew that look. She was weighing up how to broach something with him.

"Oh, I got that adaptor for your computer, big man," she said, dropping her bag on the table.

"Aw, nice! Thanks, Mum!" He turned excitedly, wincing as the sudden movement sent a spike of pain through his ribs. Mason had really done him over.

Ignoring the pain, he opened the bag to retrieve the adaptor. Finally, he was up to date with the current state of technology. It had taken long enough. Now, he was excelling in his media studies class and had even built his own webpage. As nice as it was to have all this new material stuff at last, it wasn't what really mattered.

No, what *really* mattered was the change in his mother's life. In a very short time, she'd gone from working as an assistant in the office of his uncle's trucking company, to running the whole office! Most importantly, there were no more night shifts.

He didn't want her to lose this new spark of life the job had brought her. God knew she deserved it, especially after years of putting up with his boorish father, and low-paying, soul-destroying employment.

He returned to stacking the last dishes in the washer before hitting start. As it whirled into action, his mother patted the chair next to her at the table. "Sit with me, big man. You want a Milo?"

"I don't drink that stuff anymore," he scoffed.

"Ah, that's right, you're on the grown-up drinks now." Hopping up, she grabbed two mugs from the cupboard, spooning large clumps of instant coffee into them.

"Easy! I need to get some sleep tonight," he joked.

Tipping some back into the jar, she cleared her throat as she flicked the kettle on. "How was school today, big man?" she asked casually.

He shrugged.

"Nothing happened?"

He shook his head, avoiding her eyes.

"Well, I got a message this afternoon saying you weren't in your last two classes." Folding her arms, she waited for his reply. The kettle bubbled away behind her.

"I… I had to study," he stammered.

"Really?"

"Yeah, I have a big test on Monday and—"

"Sweetheart, you're a terrible liar."

"I'm not lying!" he said, throwing his hands up in exasperation.

"Well, the bruise on your cheek says otherwise." She pulled back his floppy hair to inspect the damage.

"It's nothing, just a stupid accident."

"Brody, how can I help you when you won't tell me the truth?"

"I don't need help!" He grabbed his school bag and dashed down the long hall to his room.

His mother gave pursuit. "Brody, please! We should talk about this!"

"I've got homework to do!"

Her pushing in front brought him to a stop. "Listen, you shouldn't have to put up with this—"

His face flushed hot with anger. "It's just how things are, Mum!"

"Well, they shouldn't be—"

"Yeah? Well, Todd and Mike shouldn't have died, but they did! Dad shouldn't have kept drinking, but he did! And I should have kept in contact with the only friend I have in this shitty world, but I didn't." His breaths came in harsh gasps. "This is how it is. It never changes. Never!"

Storming passed her to his room; he slammed the door behind him.

"Brody, wait!"

Leaning back on the heavy door, he dropped his head into his hands. He hadn't meant to yell, but he didn't want to drag her down. She finally had money, stability and, importantly, hope for the future. He saw it in her face every day when she came home bouncing through the door from work. She shouldn't have to worry about him.

*You have to be brave and get through this yourself!*

Lifting his head from his hands, his eyes drifted to the photo that hung above his bed. It was the one Zoe had given him the day he'd left the Pastures. Todd, Mike and Zoe all smiling, all with their arms around him. His gaze lingered on the girl with the big green eyes.

He knew what Zoe would say, *"Being brave, means having the courage to ask for help."* Brody could almost hear her voice in his head. He blinked as an idea came to him. Hurrying over to his desk, he powered up his computer.

Opening the message app, he typed her name. Their conversation thread opened. The last message either of them had sent was well over a year ago. Blowing hair from his eyes, he began to type furiously before his courage fled… 'Hello Zoe, how are you? I'm extremely sorry to contact you out of the blue…'

He sighed, shook his head. No, that was way too formal. What was he thinking? They'd fought cave-dwelling terrors together, and even shared a kiss once. He could be more casual, right? They were still close, weren't they? He deleted the text and started again.

'What up, Z! What's the haps?'

Grunting with frustration he pulled at his hair. What the hell was that? Was he trying to sound like the biggest douche of all time? Rubbing the bridge of his nose, he cringed.

What the hell was he thinking trying to contact her now? It had been too long. She probably wanted to forget all they'd been through. Releasing a long breath, he deleted the message.

But suddenly the messenger app chimed, and a new message appeared, then another and another. The messages that had been sent to him through the day were loading up. But why were there were so many. He scanned the screen with a suspicious eye. He never got this many. Who on earth were they from?

When he saw the names of kids from his school, a hideous sinking feeling dropped into his stomach. Pulse rising, he clicked on the first message. A video with the caption, 'You got jumped, murderer!'

Brody clicked the link. A bumpy video of Mason beating him up played.

Closing it quickly, he opened the next message. Another video, this one was from a different viewpoint. The caption read, 'Hope he kills you off next time, Webb!'

Hands shaking, he opened yet another. But this one was different. It had been sent by one of the few kids he spoke with, Mitch, who was his lab partner in science class.

'Thought you should see this, be careful, man,' the message read. Brody opened it and saw some screenshots Mitch had taken of his classes' group chat. A group Brody wasn't added to. Scrolling his eyes down the page, his breath became short, strained, as he read.

'…Kill him, like he did to his friends!'

'…I hate that little shit…'

'…#Webbmustdie…'

'…we'll bash him over the holidays…'

'…does anyone know where he lives? Be good to finish him off, little freak…'

'…we should all get together and jump him! It'll be fun!…'

Leaping up, he glanced out the window to the street outside. All was quiet, but he closed the blinds quickly before slinking back in his chair.

*They hate me. They really hate me. All of them want to kill me.*

The sinking feeling twisted around his guts, anchoring him to his seat. He shut down his social media and switched across to his webpage. Working on his webpage was always a wonderful escape from this shitty world but his heart was pumping, and his eyes kept flashing to his window. Paranoia tapped at his shoulder no matter how hard he tried to ignore it.

The words of hate he'd read online swirled in the back of his mind. *Block it out! They can't get you in here.* He repeated those words to himself until his fear began to subside.

Taking a deep breath, he focused on his webpage. His own little world. Smiling, he puffed up his chest a little. Here, he was in control and safe.

For over a year he'd run a page dedicated to all the crazy conspiracy theories in the world. He didn't really believe any of them, but they were fun to write about and people seemed to love watching the videos he produced about them.

He called it, Mike's Page, in honour of his nutty friend. He looked to the picture above his bed again. Mike's wild-eyed face grinned back.

*I miss you, buddy.*

He was genuinely surprised how popular his webpage and its YouTube channel had become over the last year or so. Clicking across to his fan message board, he found himself sitting up straighter, his grin widening. This was where he spent most of his time. The fans were always happy to receive replies from him. Best of all, no one ever told him he should kill himself, or accused him of being a murderer.

*Maybe if they knew who you really are?*

No! This was his safe space. Here, he mattered. After about an hour, he was almost finished replying to his fan's messages, when he noticed a new one pop up. The heading read, 'Are you still researching this?'

Leaning forward, he opened it and read. 'Hi, I watched some of your videos about the things in the Bush—'

Brody's heart jumped; was this about Golden Pastures? He read on.

'...I work for a company that clears out buildings before they get demolished. We've been shredding old documents at this hospital. Thought you might be interested in this.'

*Don't click that attachment,* something deep inside him said. A churning feeling wormed its way around his gut. He was about to dredge up terrors he'd worked so hard to move on from.

His palms were suddenly sweaty. Surely, he could just let go. Why revisit anything that was going to open old wounds? But with shaking hands, Brody found himself opening the attachment.

Photos of some notes, handwritten in that distinctive cursive style from before computers had become common. It was clear the sender had snapped the images with their phone.

Eyes skimming across the text, the realisation that these documents must be well over fifty years old dawned on him. No one wrote like this anymore.

The flowing letters were challenging to decipher, and some pages were clearer than others. It was only when his eyes fell on the words, *'Creatures residing in bushland,'* that he got an inkling of what he might be reading about. As he read on, his concern diminished somewhat. There was nothing here he hadn't read before about the creatures in various stories and folk legends from the area now known as Golden Pastures.

Tapping his chin thoughtfully, he read reports of an unidentified species living in the bush… people disappearing, simply walking off into the scrub to never return… items of clothing found… a person who was discovered wandering the bush, who'd reported horrific creatures living in caves and old mining shafts…

Nothing new. But he read through to the last paragraph anyway.

Most of it was smudged but the last few lines were clear. Brody bent even closer to the screen to make out the words.

'…the patient claims that he must return to the area where he was "abducted", and ensure that these beasts do not escape the bush. He holds a belief that he, and he alone, has discovered some sort of mental connection with these creatures during his supposed time with them. He believes this will allow him to prevent these beasts from, quote: "Awakening the Monarch, and bringing forth the destruction of mankind." Suggest upping anti-psychotic medication…'

The words became a smudge of ink again.

Monarch? His breath caught at the word. What was that? That was something new.

*Monarch? Like a king? Or leader maybe?*

He scribbled the word down on a pad, tapping his pen in time to his racing thoughts.

'Awakening the Monarch?' Could that have referred to the leader of the creatures they'd destroyed? He realised there was one more page and scrolled on.

His jaw dropped.

A photo, like a police mug shot. The face gazing back at him blankly was immediately recognisable.

"Pete!"

This was the same photo the police had shown him when he was in hospital after the fire. The realisation came like a slap to the face. This must be Pete's patient report, from his time in the psychiatric hospital. Brody jumped back on to his message board to contact the sender.

'Where did you get this?' he typed quickly.

The dam holding back the memory of the death of his friends began cracking. Tears built behind his eyes, but the chime from his messenger app brought him out of his pain. He read breathlessly, lips mouthing the words.

'We we're clearing out files in an old psychiatric hospital. I was super excited when I read it. I'm such a big fan of your channel!'

'Is there more?' Brody typed.

The chime was immediate, 'No, it's all been destroyed. The hospital has been shut for ages, and all those patients are long dead. I just couldn't believe it mentions those creatures you did the videos on! Was it helpful?'

'Yes, it was very interesting,' Brody responded professionally. He didn't want to give away the whirl of emotions stirring within him.

'Don't tell anyone I sent it to you! We were not supposed to read them, just destroy them.'

'Don't worry, I'll keep it all secret.'

He moved to log off when another message chimed through from the mystery sender. 'Can you tell me anything else about this guy and these monsters?'

Brody scratched at his head in thought, then typed, 'Like what?'

'Does this have anything to do with those kids that lost their friends in the fire? Do you know anything about what really happened to them?'

Breathing slowly, he felt an odd anxiety shoot through him. How could this person be making a direct connection between Pete, and the death of Mike and Todd? Did they know who he was? For a moment, he just sat there, hands hovering over the keyboard. This person knows something, or at least they suspected, but how could they know?

He let out a long, calming sigh. No. It wasn't possible. The threats from the kids at school had put him on edge, that was all.

They couldn't know who he was. He'd put a lot of effort into covering up his identity and no one had worked it out yet. Also, it wasn't a huge leap for someone who followed his channel and webpage to make that connection. After all, both incidents happened in the same area. Just another curious fan.

He typed, 'I think it just shows that stories about these creatures have been around for a long time, that's all.'

'You don't think there could be a connection? You seem to know a lot about what happened down in Golden Pastures. I thought you might know more than what you put in your videos.'

Now Brody did eye the screen suspiciously. That question felt a bit direct, but Brody reminded himself that most of his video chat feeds were filled with people trying to connect these mysteries. He brushed it off. 'I've just done a lot of research into it, that's all.'

Thanking the sender and offering them a free six-month subscription to his exclusive member's only content, he logged off before the sender could ask anything else.

Finally offline, he skimmed through the report again. If only he'd had the chance to talk to Pete properly about his past. Where had he come from? How had he discovered the power that had brought him such long life? Pete was still an enigma. One Brody knew he would never truly understand.

Running a hand through his hair, another despondent sigh escaped him. None of it mattered though. Pete was gone, his friends were gone. Most importantly, those… *monsters* were gone. And yet, his eyes drifted to the one word scrawled on his pad.

Monarch.

A knock came at his door. Quickly covering the pad, he spun around to face his mother as she timidly entered.

"Can I come in, big man?" she asked, sticking her head around the door.

"I don't need to talk, Mum, I'm fine, really. I just have a lot of homework and—"

"I got another message today," she blurted.

Brody slumped. "What have I done now?"

His mother looked away, playing nervously with a strand of hair as she spoke. "It was… it was from your dad," she said simply.

Now the sinking feeling really did hit his gut.

She moved to sit on his bed, her hands rubbing at her arms like the temperature had plummeted, and she offered a nervous smile. "He... he wants to see you."

Silently he weighed up his mother's news, hands going cold.

"You don't have to see him if you don't want to," she said. "I'm the last person that wants anything to do with him, but he's been doing a lot better recently. His counsellor says he's even given up drinking—"

"Oh, and I suppose we should give him a pat on the back for that, should we?"

His mother raised her hands to calm him. "I know how you must feel, big man, believe me—"

"No, Mum, I don't think you do," he said, slamming his hand on the desk. "He's nothing but a loser and a bully," he hissed. "I hate him!"

For a moment, the words hung in the air between them. His mother stood and moved to embrace him.

"Just leave me alone, please!"

Her eyes gave away her hurt. The last thing he wanted to do was upset her. However, with the report about Pete and the creatures, the memories of his friends, Mason, and the other kids at school; and now to top it all off, the giant wanted back in his life?

The fluttering of nerves danced in unison with the thoughts swirling in his head. It was all too much.

His mother opened her mouth as if to speak then stopped, hugged him briefly, and left.

Brody sat in the silence. Again, his eyes fell to the picture above his bed. He spun in his chair and opened the message he'd struggled to write to Zoe. Taking another deep breath, he let his fingers glide across the keys without hesitation or thought.

'Hi Zo, how are you? It's been too long. Can we chat?' He hit send before he could hesitate, then held his breath until he felt he'd pass out, waiting for a response.

The word, 'Seen,' appeared next to his message. Brody's heart almost beat out of his chest at the sight.

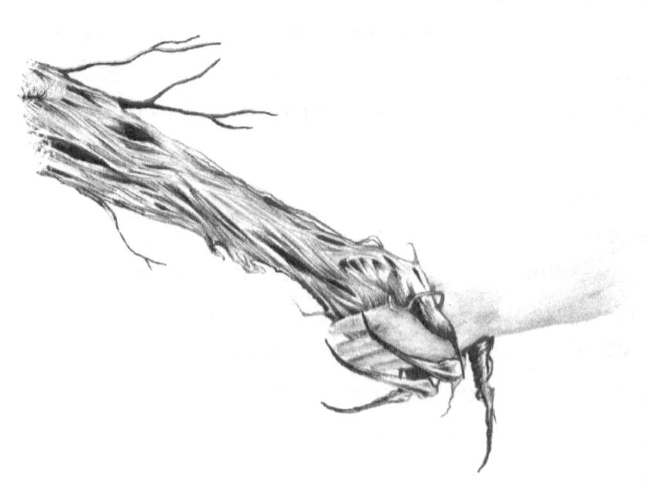

# 7

Hair whipping about her like a kite caught in a gale, Jordan sped through the streets of Golden Pastures astride her bike. Skidding to a stop at the bottom of her driveway, she dismounted with a groan. Hobbling and hissing with each step, she wheeled her bike toward the open garage.

Her legs had taken a barrage of kicks at training; she could feel the bruises developing. *Whatever doesn't kill me…*

Parking her bike inside, she reached for the button to close the roller door but paused, hand outstretched and hovering as her gaze fell to the dark street.

In the falling night, the street looked… different.

The pale punches of light from the streetlamps gave the scene an eerie greyness that was absent during the day. It was like watching an old black and white horror movie. Her eyes wandered to the empty plots of land just down from the house.

The lonely streetlamp cast a faltering glow across the swaying grass, and in the darkness beyond, she could just make out the gnarled gum trees of the bushland. Since they'd arrived here, she hadn't paid the bush any mind, but that warning the rich girl had given about people going missing had been oddly disturbing. A ripple of fear passed down her body. Swallowing, she noticed the trembling in her hands.

As much as she would never admit it to anyone, over the last day or so, she'd felt a certain energy emanating from the bush. Like someone was just watching and… waiting.

It felt familiar. It felt like Barnsford.

Steadying her breath and clenching her hands into tight fists, Jordan glared into the darkness. The trees continued to sway innocently, and the grass of the empty plots swished back and forth in a disinterested rhythm.

Thumping the button to close the garage roller door, she let out a dismissive huff. *You're being paranoid. Get a grip, for God's sake!*

The night was shut out as the roller door grumbled closed with a resounding clang. Dumping her bag as she headed to the kitchen, the din of the television from the living room assaulted her ears. A sudden, booming laugh drowned out the racket. She grinned at hearing the familiar guffaw.

Looking into the living room she saw Uncle Henry and Lilly playing a card game on the coffee table. Two boxes of pizza open next to them.

Lilly laughed breathlessly while their uncle made faces at her from across the low table.

Tall and wiry, with a body showing evidence of a life spent toiling in the sun; rough and crusty hands, from all the years of labouring, and a bright smile perpetually plastered on his face, Henry was larger than life.

He reminded Jordan of a clown out of his make-up.

Much to Lilly's amusement, he stuck two of her pencils up his nose before his expression took on a look of delight upon seeing Jordan leaning against the doorframe.

"Jordy! We've been waiting for you!" He leapt up to trap her in a crushing embrace. "Want pizza? You'll need it after all that arsess kicking at the gym."

"You know I don't eat that crap anymore," she said, wrestling herself free from his clutches.

Turning to Lilly, he signed, 'Jordan doesn't like pizza anymore!'

Lilly grinned, and signed back, 'More for me.'

Henry's booming laugh rocked the walls. He followed as Jordan headed back into the kitchen. "Oh, come on," he coaxed, "You can have one slice, surely?"

Retrieving a container from the fridge, she popped the lid, holding it out to him.

He peered at the contents suspiciously. "Looks like vomit. Bloody smells like it too!"

"I made it earlier today," she said, stuffing the container into the microwave. "It's got the exact amount of protein and carbohydrates I need post training—"

"Aw, turn it up, Jordy!" He threw his hands up in frustration. "You're a kid, for crying out loud! You don't have to live like you're in the bloody army."

"I need to stay strong and alert."

He slumped. "Fine, eat whatever. But listen, why don't you play some cards with Lilly and me? I think she's a bit bummed she doesn't get to play with you much."

Jordan glanced to see Lilly clearly attempting to read their lips without being spotted. A touch of guilt bit at her. "I was a little rough on her today," she said. Her brow furrowed in thought. Could she let her guard down for one night? Surely one night was ok, wasn't it?

The memory of the horrors of Barnsford slashed through the idea. Her eyes hardened and her muscles tensed. She just couldn't escape that place. The sight of her failure to protect her family... that would never happen again. "No, I have to do my stretching, or I'll be too sore to train tomorrow."

Henry's jovialness dropped. His voice became soft yet pointed. "Jordy, you're a teenager. Act like one for a change. I know what you went through was bloody horrible—"

"Do you?" She glared up at him. "We almost died! Our brother, *your* nephew, will probably be in that fucking psych hospital forever. And all because I couldn't protect him. I won't let that happen again!"

Silently they glared at each other for a moment. The microwave dinged, happily, breaking the tension.

Gently, he pushed a lose strand of pink hair behind her ear. "Listen, love, what happened in that town it... it wasn't your fault. Those people were crazy. Nothing is going to happen to either of you again, I won't let it."

Rubbing her eyes, she forced a smile for him. "I know. I'm sorry."

He pinched her cheek playfully but then he lent close, his voice conspiratorial. "The stuff Lilly told the police, about this demon thing... This might be a stupid question but... well, was any of it... real?"

Swallowing hard, she tried her best to act casual and dismissive. She wanted to tell him the truth of what had happened in that insidious town. Instead, she forced a chuckle. "Of course not," she said. "Look, I guess it seemed real to her. But the truth is, they were just crazy old people. Like you said."

He nodded thankfully, a relived smile splitting his lips.

She grinned up at him. "You'd have fit right in, UncleHenry!"

The booming laugh returned, and he slapped his knee. "You're a bloody cheeky one, Jordy! Now come on! Play one game with us at least?"

Seeing Lilly walking over to the window and gazing forlornly into the gathering darkness caused her to soften. "Well… Maybe I could just have one slice of pizza, and a game or two."

Throwing an arm around her shoulders, Uncle Henry led her through to the living room. "You're a good kid Jordy."

Lilly turned to face them. The poor kid looked so lonely. Her earnest face gave it away. She hadn't met any new kids her own age around here, and school was still a ways off from starting. Jordan had to admit that she hadn't exactly been much fun to be around recently.

'Are you ok?' Jordan signed.

Lilly nodded. 'I thought my new friend might be out there,' she signed back.

"Friend?" Henry said.

"I think she means this older girl she met down the street today."

"Oh! Well, I think it's getting too late for anyone to be out there now. So come on girls, pizza won't eat itself!"

Taking Lilly's hand, Jordan led her little sister from the window but as she did, she felt that strange sensation coming from the direction of the bush. A shiver went down her spine despite the heat. Why was the thought of the bush having this strange effect on her? It was just bushland! The whole estate was surrounded by it.

Releasing Lilly's hand and stalking back to the window she yanked the curtains closed, shutting out the night. Yet still, the sensation lingered.

8

It was nice to see that cheerless expression often plastered on Jordan's face, disappear for a short while. When Jordan was happy, Lilly felt happy too.

But after a brief while, her mind was drawn to the window. Glimpsing the gloomy night through the small gap in the curtains, she sensed that spark in the void from earlier. Closer? Yes! It felt like it was drawing itself to her. With a steadying breath, Lilly sent a guarded thought into the void.

*Is someone there?*

Nothing.

Even in the warm company of her family, the loneliness gripped her. It felt strange to feel empty and distant, even in a room with others.

Then a spark flashed blindingly through her mind's eye. Yet in an instant, it was gone. With a breathless gasp of exhilaration, she reached for Jordan. She had to tell her what had happened. But Lilly paused; hand still outstretched to her sister.

*If I tell her I looked in the void, she'll be angry. I must find out what it is first.*

Lilly dropped her hand and watched as Jordan bit into her third slice of pizza, laughing as the topping slipped through her fingers.

*For once, she's happy. If I tell her, I'll ruin it.*

No, she would not tell Jordan yet. She turned her gaze from the black of the summer night beyond the curtained window and wondered, *who is out there?*

he creatures pressed forward, the Seeker leading. With the warm night air caressing their rough skin, they hurried toward the edge of the expanse that housed the humans. Without warning, the Seeker tumbled to an abrupt halt, hissing in agitation.

*What?* the creature demanded, driving its thoughts into the Seeker's vacuous mind.

With a whimper, it slipped back to cower behind them.

*What is the matter with it?* its kin demanded.

Considering the darkness before them, the first creature crept forward. *I think I know,* it said cryptically.

Pushing through dense foliage, the pair slipped into a dusty clearing. The Seeker followed, whimpering nervously. In the middle of the clearing, dim shafts of moonlight illuminated an imposing human dwelling.

The creature believed the humans called these a 'house'. This was the house they had feared, and for good reason. For this was the house of the one that had escaped.

The creature grumbled – a frustrated sound at the memory. How that mere two-leg, had learned to tap into the powers that had taken eons for them to harness was a mystery.

It could only be conjectured that the human's mind had intertwined with their collective consciousness during his captivity. That time spent with them must have opened his mind to their powers. Had bestowed him with longer life than an average two-leg as well. When he had returned and built this house, they had been deep in their hibernation, awaiting the next cycle.

Long had the elder human, known as Pete, been the thorn in their side.

It breathed, shook its great head to clear the memories away. That was all in the past now. Still, it concentrated on the ruined house, searching, feeling for the elder human's presence.

*The old two-leg is gone,* it said to the others. *I sense but a shadow of his power remaining.*

It beckoned gently to the cowering Seeker, *Lead on, little one.*

The seeker tore across the clearing, heading up the hillside to the fence that marked the barrier to the human's land.

Following the winding path up the steep ridge and through the looming gums, they arrived at a rusted fence. Behind them, a light wind rustled through the surrounding bush, whistling about the creaking wooden frame of the ruined house.

High up in the spire of the dwelling, a thin spectre passed by the dust-coated window.

The creatures audibly gagged; their senses were overwhelmed with the putrid stench of humanity.

*Look at what they do to the land, it is desolated,* the first creature said mentally to the second.

*They live so close together, yet lock each other out,* it replied.

*They are violent and mistrusting,* the first creature said, squeezing the wire of the boundary fence, the metal bending sharply in its grip. *And they all stink!*

The Seeker nudged its master, tipping its head toward the dwelling closest to the fence.

*Well done, little one.*

Focusing on the dwelling, the first opened its mind to the void, probing for that spark of human energy they had sensed when deep below the earth. It hissed excitedly. There it was! That human mind pulsed with astonishing radiance. This was something very special, this mind could open many doors for them – quite literally. And yet, it sensed a protective wall encasing that energy, preventing any direct contact. As it had in the caves, it focused all its mental strength on the light, sending out the simple message: *Join us. Join us. Join us!*

The words swam through the void to the sparkling, young mind. Energy flickered weakly in response, but the defensive wall around it held firm.

Tilting its head in consideration, the first creature sat back. So, it was aware of them, but their call was not penetrating like it usually did with other humans. This mind was strong, extremely strong. A smirk crossed its lips. This was good. This was what they had hoped.

*Never have I sensed a human mind like this! We have not the power to breach its defences.* The first turned, eying its kin. *We must wake the Monarch.*

The other shot a nervous glance. *That is not something to be done lightly,* it replied, a tremble running through its body.

*And yet, what option do we have? We cannot reach that mind.*

The pair stared at each other for a time, before sharing a timid nod of agreement.

Twisting toward the expansive bushland, their joint consciousness weaved its way down into the deep caves. Together, they pressed their thoughts to the depths where the Monarch slept.

The warm air stilled, and the sounds of the many animals fell to silence. Then with a sudden rush, the bush came alive with strange, unseen energies, burning and crackling in the atmosphere around them.

So bright did the Monarch's mind burn within the mental void, that the creatures fell back against the fence and collapsed in subjugation.

*Lord, please awaken,'* the first creature whimpered. *See what we have found! We beg guidance. How do we breach this mind's defences? This human could be a powerful tool to bring forward our plans. Do you hear us?*

The creatures held their breath, waiting for a response. To them, it felt like the bushland itself were drawing breath to speak. Their answer finally came rumbling across the mental void.

*My body may be at rest, but my mind follows you within my dreams. You have done well, my children. You were right to wake me. For I, too, have felt the energy of this soul. Young in years, yet weary with burden of abilities it does not understand. Lonely and isolated by its power.*

They could feel the Monarch's thoughts probing the two-leg's mind.

*Trust through deception is the key. I have sensed this path in my dreams. I shall weave a way through this mind's fortitude with trust, you shall see. I am waking, and we are rising. Retreat now yet maintain your vigilance.*

Then the elder's thoughts blinked out in the space of a breath.

The void went dark.

They bowed their heads toward the bush as the Monarch's mind slid back to its dreams and plans.

*Come, let us return to the caves and-*

"Hello?"

Wheeling in unison to the voice, and dropping low, they slunk back from the fence and into shadow.

"Hello? Is… is someone out there?"

Peering over the long grass, they hissed excitedly. Standing beneath the light in the grass and dirt, was a plump and sweaty male human, eyes flickering, looking about the area in confusion. He shook his head. "I swear I heard someone…" he muttered to himself.

The creatures' tails swished back and forth, their lips smacking with hunger. *We could put another batch of young in that fat one,* the first creature said.

*Or we could eat it?* The other replied grinning.

Its kin hissed its agreement and slid from the shadows. The weak mind was easily breached.

*Join us, join us…*

The two-leg's body went instantly stiff. Turning, he walked toward the fence, body jerking and shuddering as he tried to resist the mental pull.

Stumbling to a stop at the rusted barrier, the two-leg's eyes went wide as the creatures appeared.

They enjoyed the moan of terror, the jittering of the two-leg's tubby body as he tried to flee.

*Pathetic,* the first growled. *It won't last long.*

The second smiled, baring its crooked teeth. *It will last long enough.*

Stretching its twisted arm over the fence, digging its fingers painfully slowly into the two-leg's throat, it snatched the helpless human into the darkness.

11

*Maybe we can catch up?'* Zoe's fingers hovered over the keys of her laptop. Blowing a lose hair from her face, she grinned as the reply came through the message app.

'Sure hope so! Let's talk again soon.'

Launching herself out of her chair with a giggle, she flopped on her bed; hair falling in a golden halo around her.

It was so good to talk to him. Even if it was just online. Of course, she'd followed Brody's dumb website with its stupid conspiracy stories. It was a nice way to keep the memory of Mike alive, she supposed. Although the whole thing was a tad juvenile.

Frowning, she toyed with a strand of hair that had fallen over her eyes. When he'd begun producing videos about the creatures, it had become too much for her. It brought up the memories and the panic. A hand went to her chest; the beat of her heart quickened.

Suddenly, she was up, pacing her room with quick, directionless steps. The horrible panic built.

*Please, not now, I don't want to think about it!*

But waves of memory crashed upon her. Todd's ruined body hanging in the cave. Mike's lifeless eyes staring at her in the dark. Clutching her head, she beat those memories from her mind. *No! Those monsters are gone! We killed them all!*

A gentle knock on the door ripped her back to the present. "Zoe?" Her father's voice. "Is everything all right?"

"Just a sec, Dad!" She returned to her desk, taking a steadying breath. "Come in?" she called in as calm a voice as she could fake.

The door clicked open, and a flabby face peered in. "You ok, Bella?" her father asked.

Zoe was surprised to hear him call her that. He hadn't called her Bella since she was a kid.

Her dad was almost as wide as he was tall, with heavy eyes and thin, greying hair matted to his head. He was looking a damn sight older than his fifty-six years.

She threw on her practised smile. "I'm fine, Dad, was just mucking around on the computer."

Forcing his own smile back, he shuffled into the room, his trepidation painfully obvious in his eyes. "How was Doctor Vasakas?"

She shrugged. "It was ok, I guess—"

"I'm sorry, Bella," he blurted abruptly. "I let you down in the past. I… I wasn't there when I should have been. I… I…"

Now it was her turn to shift awkwardly. "It's fine, Dad. Really."

Easing his huge bulk on to her bed, he patted the spot next to him. She joined him.

"I've thought about this a lot recently," he said, rubbing his hands back and forward on his knees. "After your brother passed I… well, I guess I didn't recognise that you were dealing with it too and…" He shifted, her bed straining beneath them as he rubbed his temples. "I just want you to know that I'm here for you. Understand? If you ever need anything…"

Zoe took his hand and offered her best reassuring smile. "I have Tanya for that," she joked, pronouncing the name in that annoying way the doctor did.

He frowned. "Who?"

"The doctor, that's how she says her name."

"Tar-ni-ya?" He said the name as if it were sour food in his mouth. Raising an eyebrow, she nodded.

Laughter burst from the two of them, and for a moment Zoe forgot about the things in the bush, her fallen friends, and the loneliness of life at school. When the laughter died away, her father struggled to standing. "Listen, I thought maybe we could go for dinner or something?" he asked hopefully. "I know it's not the most exciting thing for a teenager—"

"I'd love that." She hopped up, patting his bulging stomach as she did. "I think I should choose the place though."

"Gee, you're as bad as your mother," he grumbled. "She's got me on bloody rabbit food again."

"Well maybe *she* could book the place," Zoe teased. "Keep you honest, huh Dad?"

His smile wavered, and Zoe's eyes dropped to the floor with realisation. "She's not coming," she stated flatly.

"I'm sorry, Bella, but you know how hard she works, and…well…"

"Of course!" she said quickly, hiding once again behind her fake smile.

He nodded ruefully. "Well, I'll leave you to it. Don't stay up too late."

The moment the door clicked shut behind him, she felt that flutter of panic again. She really wished she'd kept that prescription from Tar-ni-ya now. But what did it matter? Her mother was busy, so what? It's not like she ever saw her anyway.

Things were fine. She was fine.

*Everything is fine!*

Jumping back in front of her computer, she clicked the message icon. Her recent chat with Brody filled the screen.

'Are you still up?' She typed, watching the curser flash expectantly on the screen for a minute. *Everything is fine.* Snapping the laptop shut she switched off the light and curled up in bed.

The panic curled up with her.

# 12

illy jerked awake, fear and confusion written in her eyes as they searched the darkness. Sweat ran down her forehead. Her breathing was light and fast. Throwing off the covers and slipping out of bed before fear could stop her, she steadied herself.

Something was probing her mental defences. *I must know what is out there.*

Emboldened by her curiosity, she slipped from her room and stole down the hall to the front door of the house. She had a strong sense of where this new presence was emanating from. Its energy flashing like a beacon in fog.

Looking for any sign Jordan or Uncle Henry might have heard her, and finding none, she reached for the door handle. Easing it open, she stepped outside.

Only the weak glow of streetlamps punctured the grim night. The moon hid behind grey clouds. The air still. Like the night was surprised by her sudden appearance.

She gently pulled the front door shut, ensuring she wasn't locked out. Allowing the void to open in her mind, she cast a mental glance to her sister, finding her deep in sleep. Touching her sister's mind caused a shudder; it was a bubbling cauldron of emotions. Lilly didn't even attempt to decipher them. Jordan's inner world was a mystery she just couldn't crack.

There was no point attempting to sense if Uncle Henry was awake. He always slept like a log. Sometimes, she could even feel the vibrations of his snoring in her room. It was one of the few times she was happy to be deaf! Redirecting her mind's focus, she concentrated on the dense area of bushland beyond the fence.

Wrapping her arms around herself despite the heat, she tiptoed down the driveway to the street. A sudden gust of wind seemed to push her toward the empty plots, and the weak glowing streetlamp.

Knotting her brow in concentration, her mind searched the void. She yearned to find someone… or something that would be her friend, so lonely was the world for her. She had Uncle Henry, and Jordan of course, but she was at the mercy of her sister's mood swings, and Uncle Henry couldn't be expected to be her only playmate. He had grown-up responsibilities to deal with.

Throwing her mind wide to the void, she padded cautiously toward the bush. The wind died, and the unforgiving bitumen road gave way to the brittle grass of the empty plots.

High above the grey clouds cleared. A slither of moon peered down at her.

*Hello?* She sent her feelings out into the void, open and welcoming. But nothing replied. *Is anyone out there?*

Nothing.

*You're imagining it all,* she chided herself. Turning morosely back to the house, she built up her mental wall of protection as she went. Although she didn't know why she bothered.

*There's nothing out there. You'll always be alone. Just a stupid deaf kid no one wants. Stupid! Stupid… a stupid little kid.* Wiping the growing tears from her eyes, she padded toward home.

A spark of energy pierced her being. With a gasp she spun back to the bush, her protective walls falling away.

There!

A thin speck of light danced on the mental horizon. Something *was* there! She wasn't alone!

Lilly giggled ecstatically to herself. But then the spark faded and was gone. The void was empty again. She waited expectantly for a few moments, butterflies fluttering about her tummy. But the void was silent. Dashing back to the house, she grinned happily.

*What is out there?*

Tiptoeing through the door, she pressed it shut and crept to her bedroom. Her call into the void had been answered!

Clambering back into bed, she eventually drifted to sleep, hope glowing in her heart.

***

Beneath the bushland, the Monarch turned its attention away from the bright light of the little two-leg. The time to rise could be closer than hoped; and with the rising came their long-awaited vengeance.

*Soon,* it mused, *very soon.*

# 13

Singing gently along to the music pumping through her headphones, Zoe offered a cheerful nod to the sun above as it burned away the previous night's anxiety.

*You sure, it's just the sun? Wouldn't have anything to do with a certain boy who messaged you last night?* She scoffed. Sure, she liked Brody. But not like that. Still, their bond was more than some stupid summer crush. They'd faced down horrors that shouldn't even exist!

Her smile fell away. The anxiety was creeping up on her again, like a spider closing in on a fly trapped in its web. Every time the creatures entered her thoughts, the panic threatened to rear its ugly head again.

Pumping the music's volume, she quickened her pace. They had defeated those horrible things. She must keep reminding herself of that.

Upon rounding a corner, she slowed to a stop, pulling her headphones down around her neck. The street before her was packed with residents, all facing in the same direction. The only time she could recall the streets being this busy was the day that hiker's body had been found two years ago.

*And when Todd went missing.*

Casting her eyes over the crowd, she saw the hilly bushland behind the houses. A rush of dizziness assaulted her. The sweat on her neck began flowing like a river, and it wasn't from the heat.

Roughly a hundred meters down the road were the empty plots. Police and rescue workers scurried about, lugging equipment, yelling, and pointing in a show of organised chaos.

*No… It can't be! It just can't be!*

An elderly woman stood in her front yard, concerned eyes scanning the scene.

"Excuse me," Zoe called urgently. "What's going on?"

"Looks like someone went missing in the bush again," the woman replied. Her grave expression fixed on the fence line.

"Do they know who?"

"Some young bloke from up the road. I heard they found his stuff by the fence, but no sign of him."

Without another word, Zoe turned, springing back up the street. *It can't be… It just can't be!* Hands fumbling in her pocket, she ripped her phone out and opened her messages. *Must tell Brody!*

'I need to talk to you, now!'

A hand landed on her shoulder, and she yelped in surprise. "I thought it was you," said a smooth, familiar voice behind her.

Tensing, she turned and forced her smile. "Detective Saunders."

"In the flesh." He straightened his tie as he spoke. Tall and dark haired, Saunders' expression was always annoyingly calm.

He looked the same as when she'd first met him two years ago, when he was leading the investigation into Todd and Mike's disappearance. Not a bead of sweat slid down his face, even though he was standing in a black suit under the roasting noon sun.

"Nice to see you after all this time. You've grown back your hair! You look somewhat presentable again."

"I see you've lost a bit of yours," she replied sharply.

He grinned, rubbing his slight balding patch. "I do miss our little sparring sessions, Miss De Rosso."

But she was in no mood for games. "What happened?"

Saunders gazed back to where the rescue units were busying themselves. "Well," he said carefully. "It seems someone has gotten themselves lost in the bush… again."

Anxiety crawled through her, threatening to burst out. She forced herself to hold her calm exterior.

"Everything all right, Miss De Rosso? You look very tense."

She fell back into her mask of a smile, but his gaze grew even more suspicious.

"There's nothing *you* can tell me about this, is there?"

"Why would I know anything?"

Saunders bent to look her in the eyes. "Zoe, I understand that things have been rough for you. But you and I both know you weren't honest about what happened in those caves."

"I told you everything—-"

He raised a hand, silencing her. "Did you know that right after the fire you escaped from, two rescue workers went missing? And we never could find the bodies of your friends. Now someone just wanders off after all this time, right when you return to Golden Pastures. So, I'll ask again. Anything you can help us with?"

Defiantly, she shook her head.

"You know, Zoe," he said after a long moment. "Spotting lies is my job."

Doing her best to hold his searching glare, she was about to retort but, in the end, she dropped her eyes.

He waved her away with a sigh. "Go on, we'll continue this soon enough, I'm sure."

Mumbling a goodbye, she rounded the corner for home, jumping as her phone rang. Yanking it from her pocket, she fumbled to answer. "Brody?"

"Zo! It's so good to hear your voice," he said in that soft, raspy tone. "How are y—"

"You need to get back here. Now!"

# 14

Stepping from the bus, Brody breathed in the dry afternoon air. The Golden Pastures Estate sprawled before him, alien yet welcoming. The bus had dropped him at the main shopping centre of the Estate. Or, rather, what was left of it.

Looking about him, he saw that many shops displayed 'For Lease' or 'Closed' signs in their windows. Hefting his bag over his shoulder, he made his way across the vast and virtually empty car park.

His eyes took in the dense, scrub-laden hills encircling the whole suburb – an ocean of green encroaching on the concrete island of the estate.

Something Pete had once explained to him echoed through his memories. *"It was their place, long before we threw up a fence and called it ours."*

Brody had flat out lied to his mum to get over here by saying he felt ready to see his dad again. He was still surprised she'd bought it. She was usually so good at picking up on his fraudulence.

Still, it was for a good cause. To see Zoe. To be there for her.

He'd declined his dad's offer to pick him up at the airport. Brody needed time to think. It wasn't that he didn't believe what Zoe had told him, but they'd burned the creatures away, and a fair chunk of the bush too for that matter. Surely, nothing could have survived that inferno. Perhaps witnessing another disappearance had just stressed her out. That had to be it. It was all the trauma of their ordeal two years ago that had been triggered again by this new disappearance.

*Or maybe, they survived after all?*

Firmly, he pushed that thought aside and walked on.

He found himself scratching nervously at his neck as he turned onto his old street. The butterflies began to make their presence known with a nasty agitation in his stomach. Finally, the house came into view.

His mouth fell open in wonder as he gazed upon a lush new lawn and garden with blooming flowers bright in the sun. The house itself sparkled proudly, having clearly been given a recent paint job.

He blinked in awe at the new four-wheel drive parked in the driveway. The vehicle was freshly polished from the roof to the rims. How had his dad been able to afford a car like that?

Rubbing bewildered eyes, he breathed deeply to settle his complaining nerves. Walking forward, he raised his hand to knock on the door when it flew open, and a pair of huge hands gripped his shoulders.

"Brody!" his dad boomed. "It's you! It's really you!"

He flashed a half smile up at the Giant as his father bent to embrace him, but Brody held out his hand for a handshake.

Not sure what to do, the Giant half hugged him, and half shook his hand. "Let me get a look at you, mate," the Giant beamed. His father had lost a lot of weight. His hair was cut neatly, and his face clean shaven. "Well?"

"Huh?"

"How are you? How's school and… well… everything?"

"Good," Brody answered with a shrug.

Silence fell, and he became very aware of his dad's nervous tension. The Giant had obviously put in a lot of effort to clean up the house, and himself.

He grinned at his dad's anxiety. Maybe it gave him an idea of how he used to feel coming home every day?

After a forced laugh, the Giant waved him inside. "Look at me, keeping you out in the heat. Come in, I want to show you your new room!"

Brody's eyes went wide when he stepped inside. He couldn't hide his shock at the interior. There was new furniture everywhere, and the old carpets had been replaced. Although his dad's battered easy chair was still in the same spot before the television.

He sniffed angrily; Brody hated that filthy old chair. All those times he'd had to tiptoe past it only to hear it creak as his dad rose to give him a whack for some imagined misdeed.

"Here we are!" his dad said as he flung the door open proudly to Brody's old room. It had been completely refitted with fresh, modern furniture. The smell of paint and cleaning product was thick in the air still.

Brody dumped his bag on the new desk turning to eye his father. "Looks nice," he intoned.

"It's taken me a while to get it up to scratch," his father said, hands rubbing together nervously as he spoke. "It got worse before it got better. After you and your mother left, I had a few mates… Well, guys who I thought were mates move in and they…" He laughed awkwardly. "But that's all over now. I've changed, Brody, I promise! I've got a new job, a really good job and…" He trailed off. "Well, you don't need to hear all that either," he said. "I'm just so happy you're here." His eyes searched his son expectantly.

With clenched hands, Brody supressed the swirling anger within him. What did this man want? Did he think they'd just brush over everything that happened? The drinking. The yelling. The violence.

"I have to go," he said bluntly.

"What? Where?" His dad spluttered in shock.

"I promised Zoe I'd come and see her."

"Oh, your friend? Sure, of course!" He stepped aside as Brody headed for the door. "Ok, well, I was hoping we could hang out. Maybe grab a burger or something tonight."

"Another night."

"Um, ok. Well, call me when you're done, I'll pick you up."

"Don't worry about it… Daniel."

The hurt in the Giant's eyes was tangible. Brody was surprised at the rush of pleasure he felt in hurting his old man. He walked on towards the front door. "The house does look good."

Pacing out into the hallway, he left his father glumly standing in his room.

<br>

# 15

<br><br>

Shoes slapping a solid rhythm on the baking-hot road, Brody hurried toward Zoe's house. 'I'm here!' He texted.

Immediately, his phone dinged. *'I'm almost at your place'* Zoe replied.

*'Just wait at yours, I'm not far off!'*

His phone dinged again, he started reading Zoe's reply, when...

*Clonk!*

He collided with someone; his phone knocked from his hand. The stranger dropped theirs as well. Voices overlapped with apologies.

"I'm sorry—"

"My fault—," said the other. They both reached for their phones at the same time. *Donk!*

Their heads clashed sharply, and he cursed with a hiss. Who the hell was this idiot? A pair of bright emerald eyes stared down at him, with a familiar smile spreading across the face the eyes belonged to.

Zoe!

Stunned, they just stood staring at each other. *Say something you idiot!* He rubbed his head, "You have a hard head! That really hurt. I mean… did you hurt your head too?" *What the hell is wrong with you?*

Without a word, she launched herself into his arms, squeezing and lifting him, so that his feet barely touched the ground.

Her curls tickled his nose; the scent of vanilla and flowers drifted around her. His heart fluttered with excited nerves. Was he really here with her?

Holding her tight, he felt the beat of his own heart against her body while the summer breeze danced around them on the suburban street.

# 16

"You've grown your hair back," he observed.

"Yeah, I kept it short to remember the guys. You know, having it burned off by the fire and all that. But I thought it was time to at least try and move on," she said.

He nodded his understanding. "I didn't realise how much I missed them until I stepped off the bus."

Taking his arm in hers, Zoe led on. Before them, the empty plots loomed. His skin crawled as he gazed at the overgrown grass ringed by the rusted fence.

Police tape was still tied around some of the trees, but it seemed the search for the missing man had progressed to another area now.

"Same as all the others," Zoe mumbled, releasing him, and rubbing her arms like a mid-winter chill had descended. "I ran into that detective. The one who questioned us after the fire? I swear he's the only one who's awake to the fact that something is happening out there."

"Now hold up, we can't be sure anything strange is happening," Brody said quickly.

"Are you kidding me? Someone walks off into the bush and just disappears. Doesn't that sound familiar?"

"I just think we should find out more before—"

"Well, you've been doing your research on that website of yours," she said quickly. "You must have discovered something… anything?"

"How'd you know that was me?" he asked, surprised.

"There were things in your videos only we could know about," she said. "You must have something new."

He let out a strained sigh, "Well, most of it we already know. Although, I did get this message from a fan—"

"Wait! You have fans?"

"I'm kind of a big deal in the tinfoil-hat conspiracy world," he said, flashing her a sarcastic grin.

"I bet all the girls just throw themselves at you." She giggled and jokingly caressed his cheek.

His face flushed at her touch, and he turned to cover the fact.

"So, what was in this message?" she asked.

They wandered cautiously toward the fence as he spoke. "This guy found a patient report while he was cleaning out this old asylum. Guess whose it was?"

She frowned.

Brody nodded to the rusted spire jutting above the tree line.

"No way!" Zoe gasped. "What did it say?"

"Well, it mentioned something called a 'Monarch'. But what that is exactly?" he shrugged. "I'll send it to you."

"Any chance Pete is still out there?"

He shook his head regretfully.

"But you never saw him die, did you?"

"He was adamant his time was up."

Letting out a defeated sigh, she pulled at Brody's arm. "Let's get out of here, this place freaks me out."

Retreating up the road, he noticed Zoe tugging at a strand of hair in thought, "So where do we start?" she asked.

"Let's start with that report," he said encouragingly. "See if there's anything I missed or—"

"Hey baby!" An obnoxious voice called from behind them.

Brody felt Zoe cringe. He glanced over his shoulder to see three boys heading up the street toward them from a side laneway. One mounted on a large bike.

"Who are they?" he asked.

"Ignore them!"

The kid mounted on the bike sped up, skidding to a stop in front of them. His two henchmen closed in on either side. A familiar dread fell over Brody. Wherever he went, bullies seemed to follow.

Leaning on his handlebars, the leader fixed them with the stare a predator might give its trapped prey. "Is this the reason you didn't want to party with us?" he said, nodding at Brody.

Zoe stood tall beside him. "We don't have time for this—"

"Shut up, bitch," the boy said, in such a throw-away attitude, that Brody wasn't sure if he'd heard him right.

But she'd heard him clearly. "Talk to me like that again and I'll—"

The boy dropped his bike and stepped threateningly toward them. "You'll do what?"

Brody pushed angrily between them. "Don't talk to her like that! What's your fucking problem?"

The boy laughed harshly. "What are you going to do, you little shit?"

Brody's throat went dry as the other two bullies glowered down at him.

"Well?" The boy cracked his knuckles, his grin revealing a row of crooked and yellow teeth.

Brody recoiled as a gust of rancid breath hit his nose, and he growled as a rush of fury whipped through him. He shoved the bully as hard as he could. "Just piss off! We haven't done shit to you!"

The bully stumbled into his friends. His grin widened. Grabbing Brody violently by his hair, he tossed him on to the hot concrete. The other two drove their boots into his ribs. Brody yelped in pain as the boys kicked him over and over.

"What the hell are you doing, you psychos? Stop it!" Zoe screamed. She lunged at the ringleader, but he knocked her aside. She tumbled over his bike, hitting the ground in a heap.

One of the boys pulled his phone from his pocket, starting to film. "Lift him up, Jason!" he called to the leader.

Jason dragged Brody up to his feet, his other friend locked him in a bear hug.

"Film it before any of the oldies come out!" Jason ordered. He punched Brody in the ribs, and a lightning rod of pain shot through his whole body.

The other boy laughed. "This is fucking gold, bro!"

Brody kicked and struggled, but it was hopeless. He resigned himself to the fate he'd endured so many times before. *It's just how things are.*

Jason, the leader, drew his fist back. "You talk shit? You get hit!"

"Hey, ladies, what's the problem?"

Jason swung to the husky voice behind him. Brody peered over his tormentor's shoulders to see a tall, lithely-built girl, whom he assumed was about their age, strolling toward them.

Dressed in black shorts and tank top, she flicked a long strand of pink hair out of her eyes. Jason spat on the ground, rounding on her. The breeze had stilled, the humidity of the air, thick, oppressive.

"Who's this slut?" Jason chuckled to his friends.

The girl laughed dangerously. "Aw, man, you're like, *so funny*! I bet heaps of girls want you, hey big boy?" Her voice dripped with sarcasm.

Jason's smile dropped. "Fuck off, bitch! You want some of this?"

She shrugged nonchalantly. "I got a better idea," she said, almost yawning as she spoke. "How about I jam *his* phone up *your* arse?"

The boy filming shot Jason an uncertain frown and Brody saw the first signs of timidity cross the bullies' faces.

"You want to act like a man? I'll treat you like one," Jason threatened.

"Oh, there're no men here," she retorted darkly.

Brody felt the energy rippling through her but Jason advanced, hands clenched. The pink-haired girl whipped out a kick with the speed of a striking snake. It connected savagely to his sternum with a hollow *thwack!*

He crumpled. The boy holding Brody tossed him aside before swinging a wild left, then a right hook at the girl's head.

Calmly, she weaved under both attacks, whipped her hands around his neck, pulled him down and brought her knee up into his stomach.

A squeal of pain escaped him as the strike landed. She slammed an elbow on the back of his skull, and he dropped next to Jason in a heap.

Both boys writhed at her feet, puffing desperately for air. She turned menacingly to the boy who was filming. He'd shoved the phone in his pocket and stood wide-eyed in terror. Stepping over her two would-be attackers, hands resting on her hips, she looked him over. Swallowing, he raised quivering fists.

"You sure?" She laughed with a shake of her head. He looked

down at his defeated friends, then turned and fled down the street. "Smart boy."

The other boys struggled up, and she lashed them with a few more heavy kicks up the backside as they stumbled away. "Where you going, ladies? I was just getting warmed up!"

Once they'd disappeared around the corner, she turned to Brody. He clutched at his hair and bounced with wide eyed amazement.

"Holy shit!" he exclaimed. "That was… you're… you're amazing!" She simply frowned down at him. "I'm Brody! Brody Webb and this is—"

"We've met," Zoe said meekly, pulling herself up.

The girl nodded with a grin, "Z-Z-Zoe, isn't it?"

Zoe flashed a nervous smile.

"Where did you learn that stuff?" Brody asked, still bouncing on his feet.

She gave him a cheeky wink, but then faced Zoe, who was hugging her arms protectively. "You good?" she asked. Zoe nodded, but her eyes were uncertain. "Who were those arseholes?"

"Just some pricks that live around here," whispered Zoe.

She nodded, flicking her fringe out of her eyes. "Listen, my sister told me you were just being friendly the other day. I was a real bitch so… sorry, I guess."

"It's all good," Zoe replied quickly.

"I'm Jordan," the girl continued.

"You local?" Brody asked brightly.

She shrugged. "I guess."

"Well," he said, "we're locals too… um… sometimes. And we look out for other locals."

"Oh? Well, I feel a lot safer knowing you've got my back," she said, supressing a laugh.

"You want to hang out?" he blurted.

She shook her head. "I better get back to training."

"What? As in fight training?" Brody kicked at Jason's abandoned bike. "Weren't they enough training for today?"

Jordan laughed. "You kidding? My little sister puts up more of a fight. Thanks for the offer, guys, but I should get back. I don't think they'll try and jump you again," she said, and headed back the way she'd come.

"Wait!" Zoe blurted out. She exchanged a brief and knowing look with Brody. He knew what she was thinking. It felt like more than coincidence that this girl should appear right when they needed an ally.

"Look, my place is only around the corner, and my parents won't be home for a while. Come over, you know, just hang out for a bit."

Jordan eyed them cautiously. "Why?"

"Like he said, you're a local. We look out for each other."

"Those guys are local too?" she said, gesturing to the direction Jason and his cronies had run off.

"Yeah, but they're dickheads," Zoe said dismissively.

Jordan laughed. After a moment's thought, she shrugged. "Ok, but just for a bit," she said. "I guess I could use a break."

As they headed off, Brody heard the light patter of feet on the concrete behind them. A little girl was sprinting after them, and waving. "Who's that?" he asked.

The child came to a halt, brandishing a large piece of paper to Zoe excitedly.

"For me?" Zoe asked with surprise. She took the paper and opened it to reveal a dazzling sprawl of colours drawn on the page.

"Oh, this is Lilly. My sister," Jordan announced, putting an arm around the kid. "Lilly, this is Brody and you know the rich girl." Lilly waved at them, and then made some hand gestures to Jordan.

Brody cast a confused glance at Zoe who mouthed the words, *she's deaf.* The two sisters conversed in sign language before Zoe asked, "What's she saying?"

"She drew that for you as a thank you. She was hoping she might see you again."

Zoe smiled. "Thank me for what?"

"For warning her about the bush," Jordan said. Lilly signed some more, and Jordan nodded. "But she says, she's not scared of the bush anymore."

Zoe knelt to address Lilly directly. "You should still be careful down there. It's very easy to get lost. Understand?"

Lilly gave a thumbs up, then turned her attention to Brody now, looking him over before signing to Jordan, who snickered.

"What?" Brody asked.

"She ah… She was just mentioning your height… or lack of it?" Jordan said.

He glared down at the kid in mocked disbelief. She grinned playfully up at him. "Look who's talking!" he said.

Following a few more brief jokes at his expense, Jordan ushered Lilly back toward their house. But the child signed something enthusiastically to her sister.

"No, Lil, you stay home," Jordan said.

The kid's bright smile dropped. She signed again. Her face urgent, almost begging.

"You're too little to hang out. You'll get bored. Just go and play on your tablet or something."

Gently, Jordan nudged Lilly toward the house. "Go on, I'll be back later."

A dejected Lilly trotted away, giving a forlorn wave as she went.

"Poor kid," Zoe said sympathetically. "Did she want to come with us?"

"Yeah, but don't worry. Our uncle is very entertaining. Anyway, come on, rich girl. Show me your palace."

Peering back over his shoulder, Brody saw Lilly standing on the front lawn of her house, watching with crestfallen eyes. He offered a friendly wave goodbye, but the child ignored it and trudged inside.

# 15

Once they arrived at Zoe's house, she led them to the back veranda. Brody could almost see their fallen friends waiting for them. How he missed Mike's goofy grin and Todd's easy smile. He forced himself to focus on the moment, not the past.

Getting them settled, Zoe then disappeared inside the house, returning with three beers.

Jordan shook her head. "Nah, I'm good."

Zoe offered him one, but he waved it away.

"Well I can't drink them all!" she said, popping the top of one of the bottles.

"Why do you need a drink anyway?" Brody asked.

She took a deep swig. "After dealing with those fuc— I mean, jerks, I need something."

"You almost swore! You're getting better, Zo." He gave her an exaggerated pat on the back.

"Yeah, been back in this dump too long." She took another swig.

"Zoe hates naughty words," Brody whispered to Jordan with a grin.

"If you have to swear every two seconds, you're not using your brain," Zoe said.

"Is that fucking so?" asked Jordan.

Zoe paused mid-sip. "Well, I mean… um… not saying that if you choose to use that language that you're a… you know… idiot—"

Jordan laughed. "Relax, I'm just winding you up."

Zoe forced a laugh and took yet another deep swig. "Oh! Brody, I almost forgot! I have a surprise for you!" She disappeared down the veranda's steps to the side of the house.

"Is this the sort of surprise I should leave for?" asked Jordan, giving him a wink and friendly punch on the shoulder.

Grimacing, he rubbed the spot she'd hit. The girl didn't realise her own strength. "What do you mean?"

"Well, you two *are* together, right?"

"Umm… no."

"Ok, if you say so."

Zoe returned hefting a new bike. Plonking it next to the table, she spread her hands in a 'Ta da!' gesture. "Hey, cool," he said. "It looks just like my old bike."

Her smile widened. "It *is* your old bike!"

He stared from her to the bike and back again. "Holy shit! It looks brand new."

"Language," she scolded, "I saw you left it behind when you moved. I stole… well, *liberated* it while your dad was out, and fixed it. I don't think he even noticed it was gone. Ol' Rusty here has been waiting for almost two years!" She patted the bike as if it were a faithful dog.

He leapt up and threw his arms around her. "Thanks, Zo!"

"What are friends for?"

"Friends?" Jordan asked with mock suspicion.

"We've been through a lot together," Brody said, with pride in his voice. "And lost a lot too. But maybe we've gained a new friend?" he smiled encouragingly at her.

Jordan rolled her eyes. But then was on her feet and reaching for one of the unopened beers. "That was totally lame but fuck it. I'll drink to that!"

Brody shrugged and grabbed a bottle from the table. "Yeah, why not! Cheers!"

Clinking their bottles together, the three drank. Although Jordan had to pop the lid off Brody's beer for him.

"So, Jordan," he said once they were seated again. "What's you're story? How did you end up in the arse-pit of the world?"

As the afternoon drifted toward dusk, the drinks flowed. Laughing with them, Jordan spoke openly with these two new friends, who were still adamant they weren't together despite their clear intimacy.

As the evening wore on, she even revealed her story to them. The passing of her parents. How her brother had taken on the role of guardian for both she and Lilly. This was something she never opened up about to anyone.

However, she left out any mention of Barnsford. It was not something she felt like being interrogated on. But relaxing in the warm evening air, she allowed herself to enjoy the company of her new friends.

Friends? Could she call them that so soon after meeting them?

She leaned back in her chair and smiled contentedly.

Yes. She could.

17

So, this was what it felt like to be drunk.

Steering his bike through the dim streets, and into a few front lawns, Brody had quickly discovered that riding while intoxicated was far more difficult than he'd imagined.

The Giant's house finally appeared through his blurry vision. Swerving to a stop on the front lawn, tumbling from his bike with a solid thud, Brody arrived.

Dusting himself off, he walked the bike to the side of the house. "Good ta have ya back, Rusty," he slurred, parking it in its spot by the fence.

Giving the bike a wobbly salute, he staggered back to the front lawn, and stood swaying as if he were a punch-drunk boxer against the ropes.

The television's glow spilled from between the curtains of the living room. His dad was still up. Brody's stomach lurched and he bent forward suddenly, mouth open, but the contents of his belly stayed put.

For now.

Throwing open the front door, he bumbled his way into the living room.

The Giant leapt to his feet the moment he entered. "Where the bloody hell have you been?" he cried.

Brody rolled his eyes. "What do you care?"

"You've been gone for hours! I was worried sick!"

"That's a first," Brody muttered gruffly. Spinning about, he headed for the kitchen, but his father pushed in front of him.

"You're drunk!" the Giant stated in shock.

"So?"

"You're not drinking in this house young man—"

"I didn't drink in *this* house! Gee, you're as stupid as you are tall." He burst into laughter at his own joke.

"Your friend? She gave you alcohol?"

Brody barged past his father. "So what if she did? What are you going to do about it?" He threw open the refrigerator door, poking his head inside. "There's nothing in here to eat! Nothing!"

"I'm calling her parents and telling them. And you are not to see her again, do you understand me?"

Brody's hand closed around the closest object in the fridge, which happened to be half of a roast chicken. He hurled it at the Giant, with a furious shriek.

Smacking into his face with a wet *slap,* the Giant staggered back, a look somewhere between shock and disbelief written on his face.

"I fucking hate you!" Brody screamed.

"Don't you dare speak to me like that, boy," his father growled, grabbing Brody by the shirt. He dragged him within an inch of his blustering face.

Brody lashed out with a hard slap across his father's cheek. "Don't touch me! I fucking hate you!"

The Giant staggered again, releasing him. His hand going to his reddening cheek in shock.

Brody felt a brick drop into his stomach as the Giant's face twisted into a familiar mask of rage. His dad whipped back his fist to strike. "You little—" But he stopped, fist falling to his side.

"Go on," Brody goaded. "Hit me! You're nothing but a bully! A pathetic old bully!"

His father looked down on him with shame-filled eyes. "Brody, I want to heal us, that's why I asked you to come—"

"Shut the fuck up!" Brody screamed, his fists pressing against his temples. "I don't want you in my life," he stated. "But you just call up and expect me to take you back because now *you're* ready? Mum and I are happier without you!"

"You… you don't mean that. You're just drunk. People say things they don't mean when they're drunk. Believe me, I know." The Giant reached for him. "I know it wasn't easy for you—"

"Oh? You know, do you?" His dad went silent. "I used to go to school and cop it from the kids there. Then I'd come home and have to cop it from you as well. I never got one day off, not one!" His voice went cold as his father's shoulders slumped. "I won't be a victim anymore." He crashed passed the Giant and headed for his room.

"Brody! Please! I—"

Slamming and locking the door behind him, Brody threw himself beneath the fresh, cool sheets, his heart pumping wildly. He'd confronted the Giant and won! At least, he thought he had. And yet, he felt the old sinking feeling dropping into his stomach.

Later that night, over the soft din of the television, Brody heard his father crying.

*Now he knows how it feels*, he thought bitterly. And yet despite his fury, he found no happiness in his victory.

18

Zoe's head shot up from her phone at the sudden insistent buzz of the doorbell. She'd spent the morning hunting for news on the latest disappearance while trying to hide her hangover from the drinking session the night before. She'd only found one report that simply stated police were searching for a missing man in the area.

That was it? Nothing else?

Again, the doorbell buzzed, and she hurried to answer it. Yanking it open, she discovered Jordan leaning on a bike about three sizes too small for her. Dressed in a black hoodie and her gym shorts, her shock of pink hair was pulled back in a tight bun.

"Hey, rich girl!" she beamed.

"Hey, what ah… what's up?" Zoe said, caught out by the sudden appearance of the pink-haired beast on her doorstep.

"I need your help."

"Sure, what is it?"

"This," she said, kicking the bike. "Could you fix it up? I can pay you."

"Don't worry about that," she said dismissively. "But isn't this a bit small for you?"

"It's for Lilly," Jordan said. "I've been a bitch to her recently. I thought this could help make up for it. Got it second-hand online. But let's just say the product didn't match the picture." She gave the tiny bike another kick.

Zoe crouched and gave it a quick examination. "Yeah, we can make this work."

"Thanks, rich girl!" Jordan said, giving her a slap on the shoulder.

"Ah yeah, no problem."

Setting them up on the driveway, she got to work. The day was bright, the sun warm, and yet the mountain winds had a bite to them.

Zoe replaced the chain and installed new inner tubes for the tyres as they chatted. Jordan knelt beside her, assisting where instructed. Zoe took the opportunity to look her over. Tall and athletic, Jordan moved with balance and poise. But when her gaze fell on Jordan's eyes, she swallowed nervously. Those eyes were eerily familiar.

She saw the same edgy alertness in her own when looking in the mirror.

"Where'd you learn to do all this?" Jordan asked, breaking her from her thoughts.

"My brother, Andy," she said. Zoe could read the next question on Jordan's face. "He passed away a few years ago."

"Oh shit. I'm… I'm sorry."

"Don't be. It was a while ago now. And you know what they say about time?"

Jordan offered her a kind smile.

"You mentioned *your* brother last night," Zoe said. "What happened to him? If you don't mind me asking."

Jordan's eyes narrowed, "Ah… It's a long story. I'll…I'll tell you another time."

Zoe let the question go, returning to her work.

"While we're playing twenty questions," Jordan said suddenly. "Last night, you kind of said you'd lost some good friends. What exactly did you mean by that?"

With a regretful sigh, Zoe tossed her spanner into the toolbox. "I may as well explain," she said. "You'd eventually work it out anyway, I guess."

"What do you mean?" Jordan asked, folding her arms.

"About two years ago, one of our friends, Todd, went missing in the bush. We decided to look for him and got lost near these caves. We tried to start a fire to signal for help." She was lying through her teeth and had to turn away as she spoke. The pink-haired beast looked very adept at picking lies. "The fire spread too fast. We couldn't contain it. Mike got trapped in the cave and… well… we never found

Todd either."

Jordan's hand went to her mouth with a start. "Holy shit… You and Brody… you're the kids from that fire? I remember that being all over the news!"

"They made it sound like we killed them. Our own friends! Can you believe that?"

"Now I really do feel like a bitch for hassling you."

"Forget it," Zoe said, hopping up, slapping the bike's seat as she did. "Done! We just need to pump up the tires."

"Awesome! How much do I owe you?"

"After bashing those creeps the other day? I'd say it's *me* who owes *you*."

"Yeah, that was pretty sweet!" Jordan giggled. The wind swept through the gum trees across the road giving the illusion of the trees laughing along with her.

"You want to hang out for a bit?" Zoe found herself asking.

"I should probably get home. I promised Lilly I'd…" She trailed off, and her grim eyes brightened suddenly. "You know what? Fuck it! Why not. But I'm not sitting around braiding your hair and talking about boys."

"Maybe you could show me some of that Kung fu or whatever it is," Zoe said.

Jordan playfully pushed Zoe toward the front door. "All you need to remember is, kick them in the nuts. That will solve most of your problems."

Zoe chuckled, shoving Jordan back, although she hardly moved the beast. It was good to have a new friend, and her old friend back too. The Pastures didn't seem so lonely now.

Sitting like an anxious puppy, Lilly peered up the street through the curtains. Where was Jordan? She wanted to tell her sister about this new presence she'd found in the void. Maybe it was just as lonely as she was? Jordan would be furious, Lilly knew that, but keeping secrets from her sister wasn't something Lilly wanted to do. Not after all they'd been through.

Picking up her sketching pad, she began to draw as she waited, occasionally glancing up at any movement on the street. But the night drew on. The street remained silent. At some point, she must have dozed off because she awoke to Uncle Henry tucking her into bed.

'Is Jordan home?' she signed.

He shook his head. "She's at a friend's house."

With a despondent sigh, Lilly pulled the covers up.

'What's wrong?' Uncle Henry signed.

She signedback, 'I just wish that I...' but she shook her head. 'Nothing,' she signed.

He kissed her gently on the forehead, and left the door open a crack so that the hallway light would spill through.

*... I wish I had a friend too...*

She drifted back into slumber.

---

*'Hello?'*

Lilly's eyes flew open! The hall light was out now, the room blanketed in shadow, but that voice was alarmingly clear in her mind. She must tell Jordan! Her sister had to be home by now.

Launching out of bed, she scurried from her room, stumbling over the drawings and pencils covering the floor as she went. Pausing breathlessly in the now black hallway, she threw open her mind to the void.

For so long the void had been lifeless. What did this mean? Where had it come from? Her initial excitement was rapidly replaced with fear. It could be that thing from Barnsford! Had it found a way back to get its revenge?

Dashing to Jordan's room, barging through the door, she ripped back the mess of sheets piled on her sister's bed to shake her awake.

Empty! Jordan was still out. Lilly clutched at her head in disbelief. Retreating to the hallway, she spun toward her uncle's room.

'Wait!'

Stopping dead, she looked about, fully expecting to see something crouched in the shadows.

'I do not wish to frighten you.'

Lilly's eyes searched the encompassing blackness of the hall. She sent out the question, 'What are you?'

'I wish to know the same of you,' the words came gently. 'You see,' the presence continued, 'I've been alone for so long. I thought you might be someone I could speak with. Few have this ability that we share.'

Lilly exhaled. Her response guarded, uncertain. 'I haven't spoken to anyone in the void since the Happy One...' she hesitated. ...that is, my parents went away.'

An emotion drifted through the void to her. Was it sadness? 'I, too, have lost family.'

A breath escaped Lilly's throat. Creeping down the hall to the front door, she reached up on her tiptoes and unlocked it. The night wind crashed about the street, whipping the trees and plants of the gardens back and forth.

As Lilly hurriedly pulled the door shut behind her, the air calmed. She stole to the edge of the road, eyes taking in her surroundings.

Not a soul to be seen anywhere. Streetlamps cast a hazy, yellow glow over the rough concrete pavement. Hands clutched to her chest, she stepped on to the street, turning to the empty plots. Within her mind's eye, the light of the other throbbed thinly.

Her apprehension swept aside as she felt the warmth of the presence growing. With light steps, she sprinted toward the long grass of the plots, bare feet pattering on the road, auburn hair flowing behind her.

'*Careful, little one, don't fall.*'

Stopping beneath the lamppost, she closed her eyes, feeling for the void beyond. '*Are you in there?*'

'*Yes.*'

With prudent steps, Lilly crossed to the dry grass. The boundary fence loomed large before her.

'*I sense you are… lonely… aren't you?*' the voice asked. Although it wasn't really a voice, more like a feeling or a thought.

'*I'm not alone. I have my sister and my uncle.*'

The light pulsed again. '*There is a difference between being alone and feeling alone,*' it offered.

The sensation of eyes upon her was strong. She looked around with a touch of confusion. It felt like this thing was right in front of her, yet she could see nothing. '*I don't have any friends,*' Lilly replied, wringing the hem of her nightdress. The admittance caused tears to well in her eyes.

'*Would you like to play with my friend?*' the voice asked. '*He is only small and gets nervous around two-legs… I mean… new people.*'

What exactly did it mean by friend? Her answer came in plumes of dust flicked up from the ground. Something was slithering out of the dark bushland!

Lilly's heart jumped. She toppled over in fright, landing heavily in the long grass. Scrambling to her feet, she turned to the street to scream for help.

'*Wait!*'

She froze.

'*You're scaring him,*' the voice chided. Whipping around, breath coming in short gasps, she looked down at this 'friend'. Instantly, her fear was replaced by intrigue. Before her was the most bizarre thing she'd ever seen.

It seemed to be part slug and part snake. Lilly could make no sense of its face, as it didn't seem to have one. It was just under a meter in length and slithered as it moved.

*'Pat him if you like. He is not dangerous.'*

Lilly reached out a hand timidly, and the creature reared up. Lilly squealed in fright.

It dropped and spun in the dirt, scooting back and forth.

*'It wants me to chase,'* she realised. A smile spread across her lips as she attempted to snatch up the creature. It squirmed between her feet, and Lilly dashed after it in pursuit.

Both skidded around the plots. Fits of laughter burst from Lilly as they hustled this way and that.

Finally, she cornered it against the fence beneath the shadow of a mighty gum tree. Spinning on the spot, it goaded her to catch it. Diving down, she snatched it up.

Lifting it to her shoulder as one might with a pet cat, she examined the thing closely.

The thick skin scratched her face, but she ran her hands over the scaly hide. It was not wet or slimy.

*'He likes you,'* the presence stated.

*'What is he?'*

She felt the presence smile. *'Come through the fence. We'll show you,'* it replied softly. But placing the creature down and stepping cautiously away, she looked to her home. Was this …safe?

The thing slithered under the wire fence, and into the shadows. *'No, I better go,'* she thought to the other. *'My sister will get angry if she finds I snuck out.'*

Disappointment could be felt from the presence. *'I understand. But you must come back and visit us tomorrow.'*

Lilly probed this new presence as deeply as she dared, searching for any hint of malignancy. But it's light glowed affably and inviting in the void.

*'I will,'* she replied. *'Promise!'*

*'Goodbye then, little one. Until tomorrow.'*

Her heart aflutter with the thrill of discovering this new friend, Lilly skipped back up the dark road.

The weight of loneliness was lifting, and she felt as fresh as the night air that danced around her.

From the shadow of the mighty gum, where only moments ago the child two-leg had stood, eyes watched it jog an awkward gait back to its dwelling. Feet pattering on the hard surface of the road, the little two-leg stumbled more than once. Waiting until it was inside the dwelling, the mighty gum tree then unravelled itself.

For it was not a tree at all but the two creatures wrapped around each other. Their minds linked to the Monarch below the hills.

'That is what we seek?' one of the creatures asked indignantly. 'It's nothing but a runt!'

The Monarch's words crashed with the ferocity of waves born from a stormy sea, battering the creature's mind. *'That "runt's" mind holds great potential! It could open the gateway to the world beyond! It could bring forward our plans for domination by an inconceivable amount of time! If we can open the gates to the beyond, we will not need to rebuild our numbers before we attack. Never question! Simply obey, and we will rise again to take back the world of men!'*

Bowing to the bush, body trembling beneath the might of the Monarch's mental fury, the creature shivered as it asked, *'But what of the boy and girl? They have returned! We sense them out there. They know where to find us and—'*

The creature winced as the leader's mind ground its force upon it. *'They believe us dead; they are of no concern… yet. But you are right, my child. We must act quickly. We shall bring the little two-leg to us tomorrow. We must not frighten it off. Do you understand?'*

*'Could we not simply snatch it now?'*

*'And what if it escapes? What if it refuses to help us? What if it tells the elder two-legs? The ones with their weapons and rage?'* The Monarch roared, *'No! It must come to us willingly, and work with us. That is why we beguile and befriend. Only then, when it is too late, shall the runt realise the truth of our intentions.'*

Giving a mental nod of their understanding, they slid into the shadows.

20

rody skidded his bike to a stop in front of the house. Bent over the open hood of his Ute, the Giant looked up and nodded a clearly nervous greeting. "Brody, would you mind helping me?"

"Just grabbing my computer, I have to head out—"

"Will only take a sec," his dad insisted.

Shrugging in acquiescence, Brody parked his bike and walked over to the Ute.

His father gave a thankful nod. "Could you hold this tube in place while I screw it on?"

He did so. Grunting with the effort, the Giant twisted some bolts into place. Brody cringed at the silence between them; he just wanted to get out of here. He'd spent the morning at the shops until Zoe had texted him. The quicker he helped his dad, the quicker he could get out of here.

His father finished his work. "Jump in and give it a rev will you, mate?"

"I don't know how."

"Just turn the key and press the accelerator."

Brody opened the driver's side door and clambered in. It was like he had control of a tank rather than a truck. Turning the key, he stretched his leg down to press the pedal.

Nothing happened.

"It's not working!"

The Giant's head appeared around the bonnet. "The other pedal, mate," he said with a grin creeping into the corner of his mouth.

Brody pressed down on the right pedal, and the car roared to life.

"Ok! Beautiful," his father yelled over the din.

Shutting off the ignition, Brody slid out of the vehicle. His father slammed the bonnet shut. "Purring like a kitten."

"How'd you learn to fix this stuff?"

"When I was in trucking, you had to learn to fix things alone," his father said. "No one was coming to save you."

"Isn't that the truth," Brody stated softly.

"How you feeling after your big night?" the giant asked carefully.

Brody shook his head. "I'm never drinking again."

A short laugh escaped his father's lips. "Yep, spoken like a true Webb."

"I mean it! I don't want to end up like you—" He stopped himself, but his father looked away, nodding sadly.

"That's fair. I was pretty horrible. I blamed things that went wrong on everyone else. It took me losing you and your mother to realise that I was the one to blame."

"Dad... I..."

"Please, mate, just let me say this. After everything you went through, losing your friends and having to deal with me... and to see you now... Well, all I can say is you're a braver man then I ever was." He saw a glimmer of hope in his father's sombre gaze. "Want me to drop you back at your friend's place?"

"I'll just ride over."

"You know, mate, you can tell me what happened down in the caves, if you want to. I mean, what *really* happened." His father looked at him expectantly.

Brody looked away. "Listen, Dad, what happened down there is not something I want to think about. I lost my best... my only friends. That's what happened."

Gripping his bone-thin shoulder, his father looked him in the eye. "If anyone can get through it, mate, it's you."

Brody nodded and ducked inside, grabbed his laptop, and returned to his bike. The Giant was fiddling with the Ute's tyres now. Brody contemplated staying, maybe spending just a little more time with his father.

No, there were more important things to deal with. Hefting his bag on to his shoulder, he rode out on to the street.

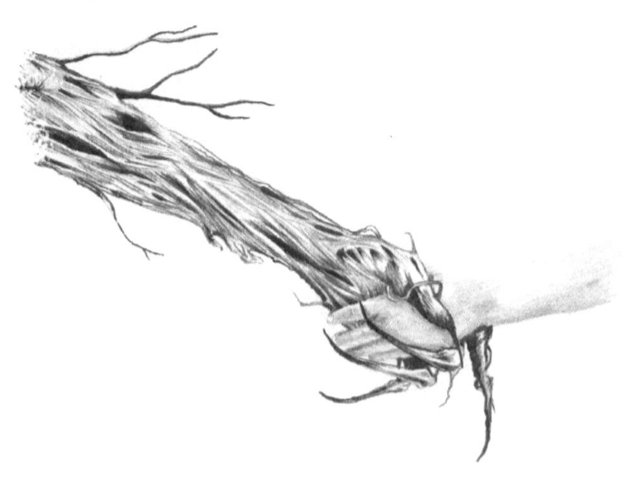

21

illy threw her hands in the air with frustration; she just couldn't wrap her head around Jordan's mood swings. One day it seemed that no matter what Lilly did, it would enrage her sister. But then there were days where Jordan had a playful cheekiness about her. Admittedly, these days were rare. However, Jordan had been all smiles and happy energy today. Whereas yesterday, she'd been grim and dismissive.

Abandoning her quest to decipher her sister's temperament with a shake of her head, Lilly amused herself by drawing a new picture for Uncle Henry. Sat on the front lawn enjoying the sun, she let out a happy squeal of surprise when Zoe appeared striding down the street, curly hair bouncing as she walked. The older girl smiled and waved to Lilly, who waved excitedly back.

Jordan emerged as if she'd been waiting in the wings, and the older girls ushered Lilly to the garage.

'I have a surprise for you,' Jordan signed.

Lilly followed. After a moment, Jordan emerged wheeling a white and pink bike.

The two older girls looked on expectantly. 'For me?' Lilly signed.

Jordan nodded, signing, 'Zoe fixed it up for you.'

Lilly ran forward gripping her sister in a bear hug around her waist.

Never had Jordan given her a present like this. In fact, she couldn't recall Jordan ever gifting her anything at all. But this was perfect. Now, she could ride around the estate with the big kids. The older girls spent some time showing her the brakes and giving a few safety tips.

Then Zoe nudged Jordan. Lilly read her lips closely, "We should head down to the park now, Brody shouldn't be far off," she said.

Jordan nodded. "Ok Lil, we'll head off—"

'Let me get my shoes on,' Lilly signed excitedly. Placing the bike down carefully she was about to dash into the house when Jordan took her arm.

'Why?'

'To go to the park,' she signed, bouncing on the spot excitedly. Finally, she'd be out of the stuffy house and get to hang with the older kids.

Jordan gave an awkward glance to Zoe. "Lil… you can't come." Her heart sank, and this wasn't lost on Jordan. "When I get back, I'll teach you to ride this thing properly. I promise. Ok?"

'I won't get in the way,' Lilly signed. 'Can I just ride around the park while you're there? Please?'

Jordan shook her head. 'No, I need to speak with my friends, I can't look after you.'

'But I need to tell you something too—'

'Later,' Jordan signed with finality.

'Please! It's important—'

But the older girls had already turned and walked off. Zoe gave her another wave. And just like that, Lilly was alone again. Watching the two older girls stride happily down the street together, Lilly squeezed her fists tightly.

Then her eyes drifted to the empty plots, and the bush beyond.

## 22

Gliding his bike across the shopping centre's almost empty carpark, Brody spotted the girls perched atop the half-pipe ramp in the adjacent skate park, a box of Cruisers between them. He sped over to join them.

Dumping his bike and strapping his computer bag tightly to his back, he sprinted up the ramp. Almost reached the top, then slid back down with a grunt. He just wasn't strong enough to make it.

He tried again, and Jordan reached down and yanked him up with one hand.

"We need to get you into the gym. Badly!" she said, fixing him with the gaze of a disappointed parent.

"Not all of us can be half-Viking, half cage-fighter," he said, slumping next to them.

"You could if you drank some cement and did a push up or two." Jordan ruffled his hair.

Zoe threw an arm around him. "He can hold his own, trust me!"

The two then ruffled his hair with a cackle.

"Stop assaulting me!" he cried.

Jordan laughed. Zoe's eyes caught his. In the moment of silence, an unspoken agreement passed between them. It was time to tell their new friend the whole story.

"Hey, Jordan?" Brody said.

She turned, flicking her fringe out of her eyes as she did. "Have you heard about what happened here two years ago?"

"If you mean your friends, Zoe told me that you… you know… lost them."

Again, his eyes went to Zoe's, and she nodded for him to continue. "There's a reason we wanted to talk to you."

Jordan's eyes flitted between the two of them, taking on that suspicious glare she'd had when they'd first met. "I'm listening," she said, reaching for one of the Cruisers.

Brody began to tell their story.

Using his laptop, Brody presented Jordan with all the research he'd collected over the last two years.

Jordan's eyes bore into him. Downing her drink, she waved a silencing hand. "I like you, Brody, and I don't like many people. But if you're bullshitting me—"

"I know how it sounds; I do! But I swear to you, it's the truth," he said; hand going to his heart as he spoke.

"And now they're back," Zoe muttered, voice laced with fear.

They sat for a moment; the silence punctured by the rush of wind through the surrounding hills.

A strained sigh escaped Jordan. "Well, if we're sharing…" She leant toward them. "Have you guys ever heard of a town called Barnsford?"

Brody nodded excitedly. "Hell yeah! The Barnsford murders! It was all over the news a couple of months ago. I tell you what, they've hushed that up, and I reckon the authorities know more then they pretend to—"

"There were no murders," Jordan said sharply.

"Technically true," he said, whipping open his laptop again, "But back in the past, all these kids were sacrificed as part of this insane cult's ritual."

He opened a file on his computer, turning it to show the girls the screen. Voice coming at a rapid-fire pace, he said, "See? I've done a ton of research into it. For my webpage. And the really creepy thing is, this one family that was passing through the town got caught up in it. They got away, but the eldest brother went crazy and—"

"My brother is *not* crazy!" Jordan stared at them with watery eyes. "It wasn't his fault," she continued. "He's not crazy. He's not!" A tear spilled down her cheek.

"*Your* brother?" Brody's eyes went wide. Shutting the laptop with a snap he pointed a shaking finger. "The sisters! The ones who escaped Barnsford! You and your sister… It's you! I mean… you're them!"

She nodded. Her eyes cast to her wringing hands.

Zoe dashed around to comfort the usually stoic Jordan.

"We haven't been allowed to see him for ages," Jordan said, hugging her knees to her chest as she spoke. "They keep him locked up like a criminal, and he didn't even do anything! *He* was the victim!" Her eyes flickered between Brody and Zoe. "I feel like that thing is still out there, waiting for me," she whispered. "That's why I train so hard. I have to protect Lilly. She's all I've got left."

"What actually happened in Barnsford?" Zoe whispered.

"Let's just say that after all the shit I've seen, I know there's more to this world than most people can believe."

Brody's eyes glared at the looming bushland around them. "Except that someone has gone missing, and there isn't any evidence that they're back. It could all just be a coincidence," he offered.

"So, we just do nothing?" Zoe asked with disbelief.

"I'm just saying that we need to be absolutely certain," he said.

Zoe's mouth curled in a grimace. Her shoulders slumped. She fell into silent contemplation.

"This house… Pete's house?" Jordan asked. "Is it that old one you can see from the plots? With the tower thing poking above the trees?"

"Yeah. That's it," Brody said.

Jordan rubbed her temples. "So, these things are supposedly in the bush?"

He nodded.

"Right next to where I live?"

Brody nodded again.

Jordan reached for another Cruiser. "Well, isn't that just fucking tops." She took a long gulp of the drink.

He and Zoe chuckled; a nervous, forced sound. *Be brave,* Brody told himself. *If they're out there, you can defeat them again.*

Looking to the gathering pale sky, he saw the beginnings of the approaching twilight. His hands quivered at his side. *Keep telling yourself that.*

## 23

illy observed her uncle fiddling with one of his machines in the open garage. The constant swearing under his breath was a clear tell that whatever he was attempting to get the machine in front of him to do, it was refusing. Thanks to her uncle's liberal use of swear words, Lilly had become very adept at lipreading them.

Gliding her new bike down the crest of their driveway and onto the deserted street, she swung it in a wide arc before hopping off and walking it back up the driveway to repeat the process.

Jordan had promised to teach her to ride this thing properly, but her sister still wasn't back from hanging out with her new friends.

Considering Jordan had terrified Zoe at their first meeting, Lilly was perplexed by this sudden friendship.

She kicked a rock from the driveway; *teenagers just don't make sense!*

The sun was getting low now, and still Jordan wasn't home. Lilly's heart sank; her sister had forgotten about her. Who could blame her? Jordan was sixteen and had real friends.

*Who wants to hang out with a stupid deaf kid anyway?* she thought bitterly.

Her gaze landed on the empty plots. If Jordan was busy with her friends, then maybe Lilly could go and visit her own. She had promised, after all. But what if Jordan came home and found her there? She'd be furious.

Her tiny fist smacked the bike's handlebars in frustration. So what? She'd probably just gotten Lilly this bike to keep her out of the way.

*Don't think that. You know she cares about you.*

Then where was she? Jordan had promised to teach her to ride. Promised!

Turning to Uncle Henry, who seemed to be in the middle of cursing at the machine again, she dinged the bell on her bike; his head shot up, and his expression switched immediately to an affectionate grin.

'Can I ride down in the grass?' she signed, before pointing to the empty plots.

After a thoughtful scratch of his beard, he signed back, 'Yes. But stay where I can see you.'

Pushing off down the driveway, the bike tottered awkwardly down the road. Opening her thoughts to the bush as she approached, she sent out a message to the void. *Hello? Are you still out there?*

The light of the presence spread like sunrise across the void. She felt the rush of warm energy as the presence reached her.

*Hello, little one.* The greeting washed over her like a summer wind. *We've been waiting for you.*

*You're here!* she replied excitedly. Stopping her bike, and leaning it against the streetlamp, she pushed through the grass. Gripping the fence, peering between the chain links, she allowed her mental barriers to slip away, and her thoughts to flow freely.

*Is your little friend here, too?*

*Oh, yes. He would love to play again,* her friend replied. Then she felt its energy change. Becoming very focused.

*Come and… join us?*

A burning energy punched through her thoughts. Suddenly, she felt an overwhelming need to enter the shadowy bushland beyond. *I… I don't think I should go in there.*

A slight sensation of bemusement emanated from the other. The energy narrowed in on her like a needle. *Come and… join us?*

Not knowing exactly why, Lilly ducked through a small hole in the fence and walked into the shadows of the trees. It was as if her body was on autopilot.

*Yes! Join us… join us,'* the other growled.

She wanted to look back and call to Uncle Henry, but her movements weren't her own.

Coming to the crest of a steep descent, Lilly became aware of a twisted gum bending toward her on one side. She could have sworn she felt a gust of hot breath from that tree but that couldn't be possible. The pull to continue deeper into the bush was irrepressible.

A shot of sobering fear raced through her body and broke the mental spell. Lilly threw up the protective wall in her mind. *What's happening?* she demanded. Heart pumping, she turned, ready to flee back up the hill. This didn't feel right.

*Wait!* the presence called. *Please! I mean you no harm. I need your help!*

Lilly's hands twisted a strand of her hair in worry. *How did you do that?*

It ignored her question. *Remember, I told you about the family I lost?* it said quickly.

*Yes,* she answered timidly.

*I have some other family who are trapped. I need your help to free them.* Its thoughts probed cautiously. *I'm sorry. I shouldn't have forced you. I was afraid you wouldn't help.*

*I don't understand. Why did you do that? I thought you were my friend.*

The energy pulsed. *I am! I sense a power within you. I know you sense it too! Your mind is—*

*—Is a gate?* Lilly found herself finishing the thought. She'd discovered that power in Barnsford. The memory of the sensation of opening the gate and power surging through her was as clear now as it was then.

*I can help you understand the power you have,* the presence said. *I can show you the gates you can open. There are many worlds beyond this one. But they are not easily reached. But I can help you be more than what you are.*

Her pulse was racing, and yet her fear was subsiding. Maybe there was a reason she and this new presence had found each other.

*However,* the other continued gently. *If you do not wish to help us, we will understand. We ask too much from one so young.*

The pull of the bush was strong. It felt as if the trees themselves were watching, waiting for her decision.

*Please, little one,* the presence continued. *Please… join us… join us.*

*I will,* she replied firmly. *I will help you. Isn't that what friends do?*

Again, she felt that smile.…*yes, that is what friends do.*

Stepping down the slope, Lilly reached out a hand to the twisted tree to keep her balance.

*Stop.*

Lilly obeyed.

*It is a long journey to my home. My friends will take you there much faster.*

A jolt of terror ripped through her as the tree she had her hand on untangled itself. Rearing away from it, tumbling over a hollow log, Lilly landed hard on the rough earth.

Her horrified eyes looked up to the tree, which was certainly *not* a tree. Tall, thin, and twisted, its skin like dried wood, two ghostly eyes blinked open.

Too terrified to scream, she could only sit and stare. Her heart beat with such ferocity that it pulsed through her whole body.

Behind a wall in the void, she could sense thoughts passing back and forth between this thing and the presence.

Regaining control with a huge mental effort, she was about to scream for Uncle Henry when the creature uncoiled its slender talons.

*Don't be afraid,* the other said. *Join us… join us.*

Lilly took the creature's hand.

# 24

A lightning strike of pain pierced Jordan's mind. Grimacing, she clutched a hand to her head.

"You all right?" Zoe asked.

*Lilly!*

Jordan's stomach turned with a hideous panic. She looked about her frantically, as if Lilly should be right there in the skate park with them. "My sister… Something's wrong," she stammered.

Zoe frowned. "What are you talking about?"

"I have to get home," she snapped.

Her phone buzzed into life. Wrenching it out of her pocket, she checked the caller ID. Uncle Henry. She answered.

His voice was a babbling mess on the other end of the line. "What happened?" she almost screamed.

There was a sudden pause in the old man's mumbled panic, then a single word. "Gone!" he croaked. "Lilly… she… she's gone!"

## 25

oe trembled violently as she watched the commotion play out. Police and rescue services bustled around the empty plots. Red and blue flashing lights coloured the night. Squatting in the gutter beside her, Brody's eyes fixed on the emergency workers milling beneath the solitary streetlamp. They checked over their kits then filed through the hole in the boundary fence.

"They're back," Zoe whispered, her voice little more than a breath. Brody didn't respond, just shot to his feet and began to pace. "Did you hear me?" she blurted. "Those things are out there, and we've been sitting around partying—"

"We don't know that," Brody snapped.

"If you say that one more time…" Zoe let the threat hang.

Chin falling to his chest, Brody hugged his arms tightly about himself.

"You're scared, I get it," she offered softly. "God knows I'm about ready to crumble but we have to do something. We must get Lilly back—"

"How?" he asked desperately. "The cops will never listen to us. You know that!"

Her anguished eyes fell to the plots. Jordan was there in the arms of her uncle, the two talking with a couple of officers.

Breaking from her uncle's arms, Jordan sprinted to the boundary fence. A policeman restrained her before she could cross into the bush.

It was all clear now.

How could they have been so foolish? The creatures had never gone anywhere. Ignorantly, they had assumed the fire had finished them off. How could they be so stupid?

Brody stepped closer. "What are you thinking?"

A strained sigh of resignation escaped her lips. "Two years ago, we made a promise to each other," she said. "Now we keep it."

She looked to the small bike propped against the street post.

Lilly's bike.

*I dared believe it was over.*

# 26

rody sat bent over his laptop scanning through a mess of documents. Even with the air conditioner on full blast, Zoe's room was a muggy furnace. They had retreated to her house to scan through the pages of research he'd collected over the last two years. Brody flicked sweat from his eyes. "There's so much to go through," he said. "Find anything?" he asked wearily. He'd given her a printout of Pete's patient report.

"I don't even know what I'm looking for!" Zoe's words came in a frustrated hiss.

"I think we might have to come clean and—"

The click of Zoe's door startled them both to standing. Zoe stuffed the printout under her desk, while Brody quickly shut the laptop. Her father's voice boomed in protest. "You can't just barge in here and harass my daughter!"

"We're just doing our job, Mr De Rosso."

Zoe swallowed hard as Detective Saunders appeared.

Fixing her with a gaze of steel, the detective meandered calmly in. "Miss De Rosso and…" He smiled widely. "Mr Webb! How are you?"

"F-f-fine, thank you," Brody stammered.

Two uniformed police followed the detective inside. Unlike Saunders, the officers were drenched in sweat from the oppressive summer night.

Saunders undid the button of his black jacket and spun the chair around to sit on.

"Now just a bloody minute!" Zoe's dad blustered, pushing his bulk past the two uniformed police. "Is she in some sort of trouble?"

Saunders looked her father over. "Mr De Rosso, I need to ask her some questions regarding the little girl who went missing this evening. I'm led to believe that Zoe and the girl's older sister are friends. Naturally, you are most welcome to stay," he said.

"It's ok, Dad," Zoe said. "If there's anything we can do to help..."

Saunders drummed his fingers lazily on the desk. "Did I hear you say something about 'coming clean' as we entered?"

A droplet of sweat slid down her forehead and into her eye. She caught Brody's gaze; he gripped his shirt nervously.

"If you know anything about Lilly's disappearance, now is the time to tell us," Saunders' icy voice intoned.

"We don't know anything—" Brody blurted.

Saunders raised his hand, and Brody's mouth snapped shut.

The detective's eyes remained on Zoe's. "Well?" he pressed.

Brody shook his head at her.

"Go on Miss De Rosso," Saunders encouraged.

With a steadying sigh, Zoe spoke.

Throughout her monologue, she became increasingly aware of the police, and her father staring at her as if she were speaking a foreign language.

"...so, there's every chance these things have taken Lilly too," she concluded.

They all gazed blankly at her, except Brody, whose eyes were locked on his shoes. Zoe shifted her weight, wishing she could avoid their stares of judgment. Yet also desperate for them to believe her, and to act! "Lilly must be in the caves. But you must be prepared. These things can affect your mind. That's how they get people to walk off into the bush. They have this power—"

One of the uniformed officers, flipped his notebook shut. "Sir, I really don't think this is the lead we're looking for."

Her father waddled to her side. "Now you listen here," he said, brandishing a chubby finger at Saunders. "My daughter has been through some very traumatic experiences, and she hasn't been well—"

The detective stood abruptly. "Explain to me how a little girl of seven would get that deep into the bush in such a short time frame? It doesn't add up, does it? Unless... someone took her there." He rounded on Brody. "Anything to add Mr Webb?"

Brody shook his head rapidly.

"Well, there's a seven-year-old, deaf child lost in the bush in the middle of the night without water or food. So, if you don't mind, I might leave you kids to your imaginings."

With a flourish, he was out the door, her father plodding behind, berating the police as they left.

"You shouldn't have told them, Zo, not like that," Brody mumbled, hands rubbing worriedly at bleary eyes.

"What else can we do?" she spat angrily. "Go in there on our own?"

"Well, we're not getting any help from them now, are we?" he fired back.

She rounded on him. "Well, what are we supposed to do?" Before Brody could even attempt an answer, Zoe's door flew open again. Her father's sweaty face snapping from one to the other. "You! Out!" Snatching Brody by the scruff of his shirt, he almost lifted the boy off his feet.

"Dad? What are you doing? Let him go!"

"This little shit is nothing but trouble. Filling your head with all that rubbish about monsters and... God knows what else!" he said, half brandishing Brody before her, he then dragged her friend from the room.

Zoe dropped flat on her bed and lay there. After a time, her eyes grew heavy. The realisation that there was nothing, she could do for Lilly sank in. Mercifully, she began to fall into an exhausted sleep when the harsh buzzing of her phone sprung her to wakefulness.

"Hello?" she whispered.

"Come over. Now!" A gruff voice demanded.

"Jordan? I... I can't. My dad—"

"I'm not asking, I'm telling. Come over right now or I'll drag you over!"

"Ok... ok," she said. "I'm coming. I'll call Brody and—"

"I've already called him!" Jordan hung up.

*So, here we go again,* Zoe thought, the phone clutched to her chest.

# 27

Turning on to Jordan's street, the empty plots stood menacingly before her. A few police cars were still parked to one side, just up the road from the plots. Keeping to the shadows, Zoe approached Jordan's house.

"Psst! Zo!" Swinging toward the hoarse voice, she discerned her two friends standing in the darkness beside Jordan's house and hurried to join them.

Once they were all together, Jordan led them through to the backyard. Emerging into the dim glow of the back porch light, she saw the look of focus on Jordan's face. The girl's jaw set like concrete, her eyes bright and focused. Brody stepped from foot to foot, hugging a bulky plastic bag to his chest.

"Where is Lilly?" Jordan demanded coldly.

Brody wiped matted hair from his brow. "She must be in the caves," he said. "She must be!"

"Take me to these caves," Jordan said, voice hushed and dangerous.

"I'm not losing Lilly. I should never have taken my eyes off her."

"Listen," Zoe said earnestly. "These things are cunning; they're insanely dangerous, and like nothing you've ever seen before."

Jordan folded her arms. "I've dealt with worse."

Brody tilted his head, looking at Jordan with a frown. "Worse than cave-dwelling, snake-humanoid hybrids with telepathic powers hellbent on wiping out humanity?"

For a moment, all was silent. Zoe glanced from Jordan to Brody.

"Well…" Jordan said with a breath. "Technically…I kicked a demon in the nuts once."

She and Brody shared a bewildered look. "Of all the things I thought you might say," Zoe mused. "That was not one of them."

A brief suggestion of a smile passed Jordan's lips, and Zoe continued, "If we go, we need to be ready—"

"Way ahead of you," Brody interrupted. Reaching into the bag he was clutching, he tossed it aside and held up a large, metal canister.

"What the hell is that?" Zoe asked.

"I stole it from Dad's garage. They hate fire, remember? And this is enough petrol to get a nasty blaze going." He flicked something from his pocket and sparked it. She recognised Mike's zippo lighter instantly.

Jordan gasped then blew out the flame. "Are you trying to blow up my backyard, you little pyro?"

Sheepishly, Brody pocketed the lighter.

"You guys don't have to come," Jordan said softly, turning to the bush. "Just point me in the right direction. I'll do the rest."

Zoe shook her head; they couldn't let Jordan go alone. As scared as Zoe was, it was their destiny to face these things again. "No, we must see this through," she said. "We made a promise."

The unspoken agreement passed between them. Skulking to the back fence, Jordan boosted them over, passed Brody his canister, then hauled herself up.

The boundary fence stood just meters away. Following it around to the empty plots, they saw that only a couple of officers sat near the trucks and equipment. Pressing on carefully through the shadows to the hole in the fence, the three passed through and were engulfed by the dark.

After a moment, something else slipped from the shadows of the trees and followed.

illy laughed joyously, her fear vanishing with the exhilaration of their journey. After much plodding through the bush, the creature she sat astride had quickened its pace as night had begun to fall. She held tightly to its head as it increased its speed again, shooting through the night. The thing's muscles twitched and pumped with the power of a metal spring, and yet it was so gentle with her – reaching back to hold her in place and slap low branches away before they could strike.

She would help them free their friends in any way she could. It was the right thing to do. *What an adventure this will be!*

From nowhere, a horrible punch of hopelessness and fear hit her. Where had it come from?

Closing her eyes, she concentrated on the sensation. Jordan?

*Do not fear.* The voice of the presence was suddenly in her mind. *Your sister will be proud of you for helping us… your friends.*

Lilly gripped the creature's head tighter as it slipped on to its stomach, slithering across the rough earth at an increased pace. As they shot down a sheer drop in the ground, she yelped in surprise. In a heartbeat, they were descending beneath the earth.

*You live down here?* she asked anxiously.

The presence gave a mental nod.

Now, the creature sped through a vast cavern. A pale glow emanated from some of the rocks, and she was marvelling at this underground world when without warning, the creature launched toward a shadowed opening in the cavern wall.

*Mind the rocks, little one.*

Ducking her head low, she felt them drop almost vertically.

*We did not always dwell this deep,* the presence declared. *Long ago, we were free to wander the land. You two-legs left us alone, and we left you alone.*

An image of the creatures roaming the bushland, filled her mind's eye. Grazing the bush contentedly or lazing on their backs, their arms stretched to the warmth of the sun above.

*Then new two-legs came. They cleared the land with fire, cut the trees down and built their dwellings over it. They destroyed everything in their path.*

Another image came to her. The creatures fleeing into the caves, trees felled, flames licking a destructive path through the scrub.

Skidding to an abrupt halt, Lilly was almost sent hurtling forward, but the thing held her tightly. Then hoisting her from its shoulders, it placed her on the soggy earth. It took her a moment to steady herself after the furious pace of the journey below. Brushing her hair back from her face and peering about the sunless cavern, her eyes began adjusting to the gloom. The phosphorus light was stronger here, giving the cave a hauntingly blanched shade.

Her summer dress wasn't much protection against the damp, frosty air, and she wrapped her arms tightly around herself.

*Step forward, little one.*

Doing as she was told, her feet splashed through a puddle. The water was surprisingly tepid. Rubbing at her eyes, Lilly strained to investigate the cavern. Bit by bit, the sheer magnitude of the space unfolded.

Stretching away into the distance was the largest lake she had ever seen. Edges of rock ringed the shoreline, but it seemed to stretch away forever. Like a cathedral carved by nature and hidden deep from human eyes.

Lilly recoiled; this didn't feel right.

*It is time, little one.* The presence's words rumbled in her mind. *Oh, how fortuitous that a seer, albeit a two-leg, should fall to us. It seems almost like destiny, doesn't it? The gate shall be opened, the Elders will return!*

What was her new friend talking about? Elders?

A shift in the presence's thoughts pressed in on her. Lilly clutched the hem of her dress again, twisting it with shaking hands as these new thoughts poured into the void.

She shouldn't be down here. This was all wrong.

The energy before had been comforting. Now, it was replaced by a hateful and malicious oppression bearing down on her mind.

Retreating, Lilly bumped into something solid. Looking upward, she saw the creature's feral eyes glare menacingly back.

It shoved her roughly toward the lake. Another creature slithered from the shadows and stalked forward, tail whipping behind it.

*Now, little seer, with your assistance,* the presence said. *We shall arise and take back the world of man!*

Lilly's head snapped back to the murky body of water. Far out in the lake, a huge bubble of air—at least fifty feet across—burst on the surface.

The realisation was a stab to the gut.

Something out in the lake was coming for her.

Something big.

Hurdling fallen trees and swatting aside low hanging branches, Jordan moved like a predatory cat in the moonlight. The strain on Brody's flushed face showed he was working hard to keep pace. Zoe called from behind him, "Stay on the track! We should be near the house soon!"

Pushing through a thick clump of shrubs, Jordan skidded to a sudden yet graceful halt. Brody and Zoe jolted to a stop beside her, puffing for air.

Before them, coated in vines and fallen leaves, was old Pete's house.

"Holy shit!" Jordan exclaimed. "Is this the place?"

"Do you see any other ancient mansions around?" Brody said with a raise of his eyebrow.

Caught by the moonlight, Jordan's eyes gave the glow of a wild animal's as she rounded on him.

"I mean… yes!" he stammered.

"It really has fallen to pieces," Zoe said. "And it wasn't looking very solid last time we were here either.

"I guess once Pete passed on, whatever strength he was getting from this place must have passed on too," Brody remarked sadly.

"You're sure this guy is gone?" Jordan asked.

Placing the canister down, Brody jogged to the rotten front door. "One way to find out," he said.

Zoe followed, but Jordan hung back, eyes scanning the night.

Stepping onto the veranda, Zoe rapped on the wood of the door. Dust and splinters fell with each strike. The sound echoed like a gong in the silence of the bush. The night itself seemed to be listening for a reply.

None came.

*He really is gone,* Brody admitted to himself. Wherever Pete was now, he hoped he was at peace. Zoe turned to him; her face obscured by shadow. He didn't need to see her eyes to know what she was thinking. We're wasting our time, no… *Lilly's* time.

Jordan's voice broke the moment. "Take me to these caves—" Then she abruptly turned to the track they'd descended.

"What?" Zoe asked, voice trembling as she hurried back to Jordan's side.

Brody glanced sadly back to the rotting door, before sprinting to join them.

"Something is following," Jordan said. "It's close."

"How the hell do you know that?" Zoe whispered.

"I can feel it."

"Feel it?" Zoe asked.

"It's tracking us," Jordan said.

"Then we keep moving," Brody stated, anxiously scanning the surroundings.

Taking hold of their arms, he led them from the clearing but then, a sound like dry bark being slowly peeled from a tree, broke the silence.

Brody turned; the sound was coming from the house!

Zoe scrambled to pick up a rock from the ground. Gasping, Jordan dropped back into her fighting stance, fists quivering madly.

Painfully, the ancient door of the house creaked open.

***

Brody tried frantically to unscrew the lid of the petrol canister, but it slipped, falling to the ground, the sound reverberating through the night with the force of a tree crashing to earth. Zoe clutched his arm tightly while Jordan stepped forward, fists shaking, breath rapid.
"We should get back to the estate!" Brody cried.

"We can't," spat Jordan, "There's something coming that way too, remember?"

The door finally ground to rest, dust drifting through the moonlight.

Then a familiar voice floated from the black hallway. "I thought I told you kids to stay out of the bush?" The words came as a strained gargle. "I see you've brought another friend. I'm very disappointed in you, lad," the voice said with a chuckle.

Brody almost fell to his knees with relief and wonder. "Pete!"

Zoe's grip tightened on his arm. "You said he was gone!"

The chuckle came again. "It's me, love. I see your hair grew back. It looks wonderful."

Zoe tugged at a strand of golden hair as if she'd forgotten it was there.

A hazy, pale shape materialised in the doorway, and Brody could just make out the silhouette of their old friend. But there was nothing solid, nothing truly tangible.

Jordan stumbled back with a gasp of terror.

"It's ok," Brody said, "It's him! It's Pete!"

"That's a fucking ghost!" Jordan shoved him away in panic, but already the apparition of their old friend was fading.

"Pete, what happened to you? Are you a… a ghost?"

Booming laughter echoed through the house. "Ghost? No, lad. My body died after we escaped the caves. It was too much to keep it from crumbling after all those years. I had used up all my energy to defeat them but part of me remained here, in the house. After all, it was always my sanctuary."

Warm air hissed through the open door, as if the house had taken a breath. Pete continued, "My power is truly fading now. I can feel my time is very short. I held on because I felt our friends in the bush were still out there, somewhere."

Brody stepped closer. "You've been waiting here all this time?"

"I hoped it was over, but it seems the bastards have outlasted me."

"Can you help us?" Jordan pleaded, although she kept her distance. "Those things have taken my sister, and—"

"Something is waking up. Something big. I can sense it." Pete's voice carried over the night.

"What?" Zoe asked desperately.

Pete's voice came like a dying breath when he spoke. "They call it the—"

"—Monarch," Brody finished.

He could feel Pete nodding. The hazy spectre had almost vanished; his voice growing thinner the longer they conversed. "They've been planning something big for decades," the apparition croaked. "I thought we'd put a stop to it when we burned them up last time, but I fear that may not be the case. I think they're bringing in some reinforcements."

Jordan threw her hands up hopelessly. "Please, we're running out of time! Something is creeping up on us and it's getting closer!"

Pete's fading voice came again. "I will stay with you as long as I can. I still have a trick or two left up my sleeve. But this time, get your friend and go. Don't try and fight them!"

The darkness absorbed the remaining slivers of Pete's being, and the night was still again. A branch somewhere up the hillside snapped.

"What the hell did I just see?" Jordan asked.

Brody snatched up the canister as he pushed them toward the bushes. Hugging it tightly, he ploughed on. He could still feel a sense of the old man with him, but that didn't do much to placate his rising fear as they pressed on into the night.

The fortifications Lilly had built around her mind were being peeled open like a tin can. The harder she battled to maintain them, the quicker the presence tore them down. Doubling over with a hopeless scream, the last barrier fell, and the presence's mind engulfed hers. Collapsing forward into the water, she reeled with the attacking energies. Everything went dark as the other's mind took control.

When she returned to consciousness, she had no idea how much time had passed, but slowly it dawned on her that she was floating in water. Yet, it was as if she were removed from her body.

*The Monarch rises!* The thought was a battle cry ringing through the mental void.

Eyes shooting open, she suddenly found herself back in her body. Thrashing and gasping in the water, she kicked to the surface and sucked in a deep lungful of putrid air.

With horror, she realised she was floating in the middle of the lake! How did she get this far out? The pale eyes of the two creatures shone as if four moons had landed on the black shore.

Her head slipped beneath the inky waters; it was too far to swim back. She kicked and kicked but it was no use. She was going to drown! But then, her feet hit solid ground!

Toppling on to her hands and knees, the ground lift away from the water. Cold air biting through her soaked dress, hands struggling to grasp on to the slippery surface.

Eyes wide with terror, Lilly spun looking for an escape. *Is it an earthquake? What is happening?*

An island rose before her. Water cascading away from the slimy rocks. The piece of land was about thirty meters across, with jagged protrusions jutting out at strange angles.

*Let me see your flesh,* the presence growled in her thoughts.

Lilly hugged herself tightly, body trembling as the realisation dawned on her.

This was no island, and this was not a rock she sat upon.

It was a hand!

*At last, I see you…* The giant, misshaped head that reared from the water was terribly clear to her now.

*What are you?* Lilly screamed in her mind.

*My children call me Monarch. For it is I who rules below.*

The thing's face was very similar to that of the creature yet monolithic by comparison. The uneven, rocky surface of the skin split wide. The massive pale orbs of the Monarch's eyes blinked open and held her with a primordial gaze. *And now… we rise!*

Lilly screamed.

# 21

rody's face was a tight mask of concentration as he ran. The appearance of Pete—or what was left of his friend—spurred Brody to find answers. What the hell was this Monarch exactly? What were the creatures trying to achieve by taking Lilly? What could a child possibly have that they'd want?

Zoe led them down a moon-drenched path, heading toward the distant highway.

Occasionally, a car's headlights would sweep the night, the drivers blissfully unaware of the horrors playing out in the bushland around them.

"The mine shaft should be down here somewhere," Zoe said between strained breaths.

They sped on determinedly, yet his mind still mulled over Lilly's disappearance. "Why would they want Lilly?" He posed the question to no one in particular. Scrambling over a fallen tree, Brody noticed familiar blackberry bushes on one side of the moonlit path. They were very close now.

"Maybe to draw *us* down here?" Zoe panted.

"It worked," Jordan called darkly.

"There's the shaft!" Zoe exclaimed. The black hole grew larger on the path as they approached. "If I remember right, it's a pretty steep drop at first but levels out."

"I'm going down," Jordan declared.

Still, Brody's mind grappled to put the pieces together. An idea suddenly struck him. "Jordan, is there anything about Lilly that's… different?"

"Brody, we don't have the fucking time—"

"Please," he urged. "We need to understand what we're really stepping into."

Jordan was lowering herself into the shaft with Zoe's help, but he grabbed her shoulder. "Jordan, why would they want *her*? There must be a reason. It couldn't be about revenge on Zoe and me. They couldn't know that we were all friends. We only met a short while ago."

She looked ready to explode with rage. Brody could see the red spots of anger spreading across her cheeks despite the darkness but then her expression became considered.

"In Barnsford," she began. "This thing… the demon, it was like it could sense Lilly, and she could sense it too." Jordan hoisted herself back up, perching on the edge of the shaft. "This will sound insane, but Lilly seems to sense things we can't. Although sometimes, I feel like I can too. But nowhere near the level she does."

"What are you talking about?" Zoe asked.

Jordan rubbed her chin. "It's almost like she's a sort of… channel. After Barnsford, she told me that her mind was a gate, that energy or… I don't know… things, could pass through—"

"A gate!" Brody's hands went to his head in realisation. "The Monarch! Pete said he thought they were bringing in reinforcements but bring them from where and through what exactly? If Lilly can sense things we can't, maybe they need her power, or ability or… whatever the hell it is, to contact these reinforcements."

Footfalls crunched on the leaves behind them. They spun to the sound as a tall figure emerged from the shadows.

"You kids certainly have vivid imaginations." Saunders appeared before them in the moonlight. He was out of his suit and in dark track pants and top.

Brody heard a click; a blinding torch beam broke through the night.

Saunders shone the torch from one to the other before settling the beam on Brody. He battled to shield his eyes from the blinding light as the detective stepped closer. "You know, Mr Webb, I did my best to draw you out online. Tried to get you talking, but you were very good. You always brushed me off. Even after I sent you that psych report about your supposed friend, Pete. A man whose been dead for years," he scoffed.

Brody's jaw dropped. "That was you?"

The detective nodded slowly. "I was hoping it might win your confidence. You seemed so keen to talk about it in all those videos. I hoped you might slip up and reveal the truth about what happened to your friends out here."

"How did you know it was Brody?" Zoe asked in amazement.

Saunders flick the torch beam to Zoe with a sigh. "I'm a detective, Miss De Rosso, it's my job to find those things out."

He turned the light, and his attention back to Brody. "Also, Mr Webb, you really need to update your IP address security. Very easy to get a trace on you." He sighed, rubbing the bridge of his nose. "I'll be honest with you kids, I still don't know what happened to your friends." He said the last word with a sarcastic tone, which seemed to suggest that he had his suspicions, and that they focused clearly on him and Zoe. "But I *will* find out." He moved toward them. "This sick little game of yours is over. Now where is Lilly?"

illy was levitated higher and higher into the air, screaming as her mind was pried open by the creatures. She fought again to resurrect her mental defences, but it was no use.

*Do you feel them, little seer?* The Monarch's words cut with the sharpness of a blade. *The Elders are coming. They sense you! They await us on the other side. Open your mind, child, and let them join us!*

The vision struck like a lightning bolt. So real, yet in a heartbeat, gone. Within this vision she saw only black stretching in every direction. But from within the all-encompassing darkness, she felt something closing in.

*How do I stop them?*

The Monarch's joy was palpable. *You cannot! Not without destroying yourself!*

Now, she felt the other's attention shift. The thoughts of one of the creatures on the shore drifted to her.

*The other two-legs are above!*

The Monarch's thoughts became inflamed. *Kill them! Do not let them find us!*

Lilly's heart soared. Jordan! She could sense her sister's energy out there! But the Monarch's energy pushed her mind back to the void and the horrors massing beyond.

But just before the Monarch's power took control of her totally, she sent her thoughts through the void to the dim light of her sister.

*Jordan! Help me!*

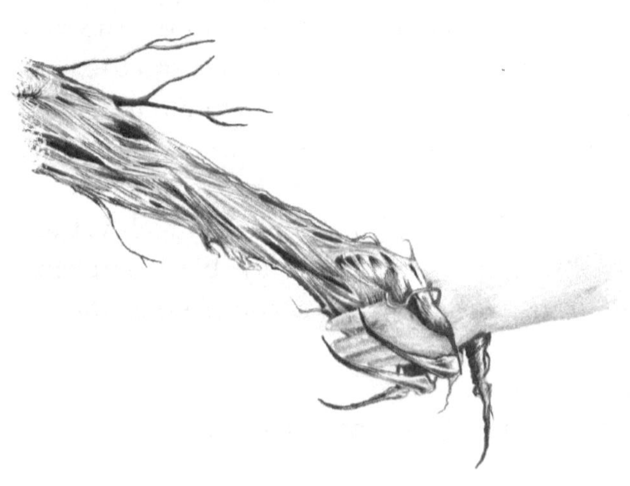

33

*illy?* Jordan's head whipped back to the mineshaft. A sickening sensation of a gate grinding open, struck her. Something uncaring, brutal, and destructive was approaching through that gate. And her sister was down there. In the darkness. Alone.

Without another thought, Jordan leapt for the shaft.

"Stop!" the detective yelled.

But she had already dropped into the depths of the mine, cold air whistling around her as she fell. The drop was much deeper than she'd realised.

*I'm going to break my neck!* But then the steep earth of the shaft was beneath her. She rolled over the muddy ground before crashing into a shallow pool. Instantly, she was soaked. The freezing water sent an icy shock to her body, and she cried out. *Focus!* Lilly needed her!

Dragging herself up on to the muddy bank, the voices of her friends and the angry calls of the detective, echoed above.

A sudden splash behind her, and Jordan wheeled in fright. Something emerged from the water. Coughing, it wiped matted blonde hair from its face. Zoe blinked up at her.

"You all right?" Jordan asked, extending a hand.

"Don't worry about me, I've done this before," said Zoe.

Another splash. Now Brody was in the water. His landing was a little smoother, but then his canister tumbled down after him, hitting him in the back with a thud. She and Zoe dragged him up the muddy bank.

"Let's move," yelled Brody. "I managed to slip him, but he was right behind—"

Splash!

"—me."

Saunders was immediately on his feet, his torch beam cutting through the dark. "Right. That's it! All of you on the ground, hands on heads. I'm done playing around!"

Jordan stood defiantly. "Lilly is down here. We need to—"

"Silence," the detective snapped.

Zoe and Brody glanced about them in the dark, true fear written in their wide eyes.

"Keep your voice down! They'll hear you," Zoe hissed desperately.

But Saunders shoved her to her knees. "Get down!" Then grabbing Brody, he kicked the boy's feet out from under him, but her friend held on tight to his canister. "Now, where is the little girl?" Saunders demanded. "What have you done with her?"

"That's what I'm trying to tell you," Jordan screamed back. "She's down here!"

"And what? The monsters have her? What a load of crap!"

A horrendous screech resounded through the cave, and Saunders spun his torch toward the cry.

Jordan saw the man's eyes widen in horror as the abomination emerged from the dark. It made the demon she'd faced in Barnsford seem like a cuddly puppy in comparison.

Sliding toward them, the terror squinted against the harsh light from the torch. Saunders tripped backward, almost falling over her. He fumbled at his belt, producing a pistol. Hand trembling, he raised the weapon.

"Shoot it!" Zoe cried.

Brody yanked her toward him. "Shit, it's got him! We need to go!"

The three hurried away, but Saunders was rooted to the spot. Eyes wide, short puffs of breath steamed in the air.

The creature turned its pale glare on them, clasping the policeman's head in its cruel talons as it did. With a violent twist of its arms, a sickening crack rang through the cave. Saunders' head snapped around to face them, horror and confusion written in his dying eyes.

The creature had just snapped his neck with the same ease Jordan might break a twig.

Instantly, he went limp, body hanging like a doll in the creature's talons.

The light from the torch was shining up at the creature, casting a towering shadow across the roof of the cave.

*Join us!* The words echoed in her mind.

Jordan's body began to seize up, but her friends dragged her away. Frustrated, the creature ripped the torch from Saunders' hand, held it up and squeezed down hard. The tool shattered just like the policeman's neck.

The cave was plunged into black.

With a roar it shot forward, and the three friends fled into the blackness.

24

As Jordan ran, a weak flame flashed in the dark as Brody sparked the lighter, illuminating their rugged subterranean path. "Where the hell do we go?" he yelled.

Zoe snatched the canister from him as he took the lead.

"Just run!" Jordan screamed. Glancing behind, she saw feral eyes fixed on her. The creature was close. Too close!

The trio bounced off the rough walls; tripped over the uneven cave floor. But pushed deeper into the blackness.

What were they going to do? How were they ever going to get out, let alone find and save Lilly?

*Jordan!*

Snapping to a halt, Zoe smashed into Jordan, and they sprawled in the mud.

The creature let out a gleeful screech as it closed in.

Brody desperately tried to pull them to their feet. "Get up, get up!" he howled.

But a sudden message had hit Jordan's mind. *Jordan! The lake! Do you see? Please Jordan, I'm so scared!*

In the time it would take to click her fingers, she saw Lilly's vision. It was so clear yet gone in an instant.

"I know where she is!"

"How?" Brody said as he hoisted them to their feet.

"We have to go down."

"Down?" Zoe cried in confusion.

Jordan grabbed the lighter from Brody, shoving them through a slim opening in the cave wall as she did.

"Down!" she repeated.

Tumbling into an open, high-ceilinged cavern, the phosphorous on the rocks revealed to her fading scorch marks on the cavern walls.

"I think we've been here before," Zoe observed ominously, as they struggled across the muddy cave floor.

Brody came to a sudden stop, pointing a quivering finger into the dark. "T-Todd," he whispered.

Jordan watched as Zoe followed his frightened stare. With a whimper, her hand went to her mouth.

Jordan strained to make out what they were looking at with such horror. Slumped against the far wall, sat a heap of bones coated in dirt, filth, and dried flesh. The skull grinned at them as if privy to a joke at their expense.

A deep groan behind marked the arrival of their pursuer. The thing squeezed between the tightly-packed rocks of the entrance.

Focusing on the void opening to her, she sought Lilly's light. It flickered weakly, guiding her on.

"This way!" Jordan sprinted across the cave as the creature closed in on them. "Down there!" A jagged opening became clear in the weak phosphorus light.

Brody launched his small frame through the opening. Zoe followed; the canister still clutched to her.

*Join us! Join us!*

Jordan's body cramped up. She froze only a foot from the opening; the creature had her again!

The monster was unable to slow, and smashed into her. The pair toppled through the opening, air hissing around them as they fell. The creature's course skin scratched her own as it wrapped her in a crushing embrace.

Faster and faster they tumbled. *You are ours now!* the creature boomed triumphantly in her mind. Crashing to the bottom, the creature took the brunt of the landing, but the impact jolted her body as well.

Through starry vision, she saw its feral eyes glare into hers. *I failed you, Lil! I'm sorry,* she thought hopelessly.

Rough talons gripped her neck and squeezed. She could not

move, she could not breathe. The creature's words beat upon her mind relentlessly.

*Join us, join us…*

The gloom of the cave slowly slipped to black.

# 25

Bang!

Zoe hammered the cannister into the back of the creature's head, the strike echoing through the cavern.

The blow stunned it long enough to give Jordan time to scramble away, the creature's mental trap broken.

Sucking in a lungful of acrid air, Jordan gasped in horror upon the scene before them. "Holy shit..." she muttered, voice trembling.

Zoe cast her eyes in the same direction. The canister fell from her hands.

"What is that?" Brody sniffled.

Zoe had witnessed some insane things in her life. Long ago she had come to accept that there was much in this world that simply should not exist. Despite all that, the thing she gazed upon now was almost incomprehensible.

A massive, seemingly endless body of black water stretched away from them. One of the creatures stood by the shoreline, arms raised and tail swishing excitedly. It seemed to be paying worship to the scene playing out on the water.

A chill ran through her body as a horrible certainty dawned on her. None of them were getting out of here alive.

The monstrosity half submerged in the lake had to be at least a hundred meters tall. Its sleek, moss-coated skin shimmered wetly in the glow of abnormal colours swirling high above. Jordan screamed hysterically, pointing to the distant ceiling of the cave. "Lilly!"

The child hovered high above the water. Nothing supported her.

That wasn't possible! And yet, she floated there like a leaf caught in a winter draught.

At Jordan's scream, the creature on the shoreline whipped around. With an angry growl, it slid forward spreading its talons wide.

Behind them another furious roar drew Zoe's attention. Despair seized her. The other creature also slithered forward, pale eyes burning with rage.

Brody snatched up the canister, fumbling with the lid as they retreated.

"We're trapped!" Jordan screamed desperately.

"The lighter!" Brody yelled.

Jordan tossed it to him.

He sparked it as the creatures loomed over them. "Stay back!" Brody screamed as the flame caught. "We burned you before, we can do it again!" He sloshed the petrol from the canister about them, but the creatures continued their advance.

Eyes darting in fear, he threw the canister at the approaching creature coming from the shore, who swatted it aside as if it were an annoying bug.

With a sudden howl of rage, Jordan charged the creature in front of them. Caught by complete surprise, the creature's eyes widened with shock as Jordan leapt in the air and threw a flying right kick that struck it in the chest.

Seeing this, Brody sparked the lighter again, bent and lit the puddle of petrol. Flame exploded into life and *whooshed* around them.

Caught in the explosive blaze, the other creature howled with pain.

Snapped out of her fear by the flames, Zoe saw Jordan throwing kicks and punches at the creature. The physical attack, mixed with the heat of the spreading flames combined to beat it back.

Zoe grabbed a viciously sharp rock from the ground, hurling it with everything she had, and watched with satisfaction as it smacked into the thing's head. *We can beat them!*

Then came a deafening roar from the lake.

All of them dropped to the ground, hands covering their ears. Even the creatures recoiled.

The monstrous thing in the lake drew back its arm and whipped it through the water. A colossal wave crashed down upon the shore, and all were swept against the jagged cave wall.

Instantly, the fire was doused. Yet despite the huge volume of water, the parched earth immediately began to soak it up.

"It's coming!" Brody screamed.

From the choppy waters, the Monarch rose.

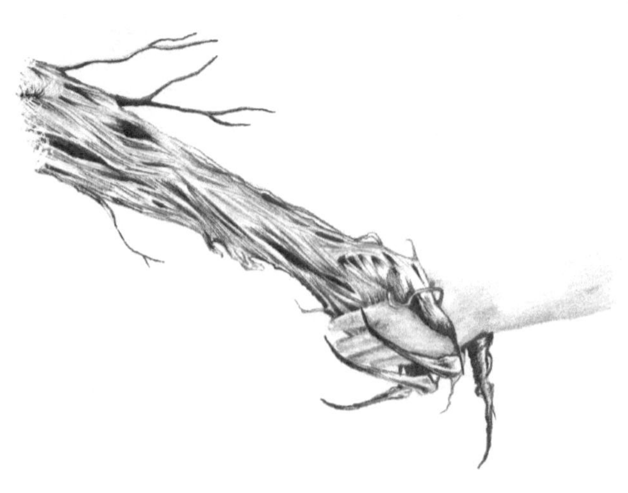

26

yes blinking open, Lilly beheld the swirling colours of what must be the gate, high above. Thoughts of these so-called Elders, echoed through the mental void. Horribly alien minds oozing malice. Screaming from the pit of her soul, she thrashed hopelessly as a vision ripped through her consciousness. It showed the Elders pouring through the gate she had unwittingly helped to open.

Their size was gargantuan, and yet their various shapes were difficult to truly fathom. Some were plump with tentacles protruding and flicking about them, others horrifically twisted and towering. There were those that squirmed and slithered like the creatures of the caves, and those that stalked on bone-thin legs as tall as buildings.

While some had clearly defined faces, others didn't seem to have facial features at all. Within Lilly's terrible vision, these monsters broke free of the caves, and carved a path of desolation upon the earth. Nothing was left standing; the world unrecognisable in their wake. Her tears spilled, dropping to the dark waters below. *It's all my fault. I let them trick me! There must be a way to stop them!*

Cruel laughter rang through the chambers of her mind. *There is nothing to be done now, little one, except for us to take back the world of men,* the Monarch said. *My power and yours combined have opened the gate! Behold, they have come.*

Her body was roughly flipped up, eyes forced open. The swirling colours of the gate were blinding, but she could make out the great shadow of something emerging.

Hundreds of tentacles swished and whipped about like a writhing mass of snakes. They parted to reveal a slash of a mouth holding endless rows of jagged, twisted fangs.

Lilly stared into the nightmarish abyss beyond the gate.

*Do you see, little one?* the Monarch said. *Humanity's time is over, the Elders have come.*

Staring miserably up at her helpless little sister, Jordan wrung her hands in a panic. What could she do? There was no way to reach Lilly and nowhere to escape to even if she could.

Bending low, the Monarch hissed; hot putrid breath almost blew them off their feet. The behemoth raised an arm as thick as ten trees, its intentions horribly clear. It was going to crush them! Her friends clutched on to her, screaming in terror.

But in this seemingly final moment, an inner calm descended on Jordan. She breathed, closed her eyes, and concentrated on sending her thoughts to her sister.

Lilly had explained once that this was how she communicated between… what should Jordan call it? Worlds? Planes of existence? She had no idea.

Often Jordan heard, or rather, *felt* things in her mind too. Like when Lilly's name came to her at random. Or when she'd sensed Lilly beneath the bush.

There must be a link between them. If she listened in her mind, then maybe…

*Lil, I don't know if you're getting this, but… I tried to keep you safe. If ever I was mean, I'm sorry, I just didn't want to lose you like we lost Owen… or Mum and Dad.*

A distant yet familiar spark of light flickered in the mental void. Quickly, it was snuffed out, and Jordan became horribly aware of Zoe burying her face into her hands, of Brody clutching her shoulder and weeping.

She looked up as the Monarch raised its arm higher. Its talons clenched into a boulder-sized fist. Jordan hugged the others to her as its arm crashed down.

## 28

Then the solution came to Lilly. Hadn't the Monarch inadvertently revealed it? The idea was a flash of clarity that was so obvious, and yet so… final. So horribly final.

*If I am the gate, and I must close the gate to stop them… Then I must close myself.*

A spear of pain shot through her mind. *You will do no such thing, little seer!*

She looked to the shoreline far below. The Monarch's arm hovered over Jordan and her friends, ready to strike but its attention was focused firmly on her.

Stabs of searing pain wracked her tiny body, and she felt her mind's eye stretch wider. She screamed and screamed in helpless agony. It felt as if her mind was being shredded in a storm of razors.

The first Elder was almost through the gate! Behind it, Lilly's bloodshot eyes saw more of the steadily approaching atrocities.

*I can't allow them to get through!*

She did her best to send her thoughts to her sister. A last, desperate attempt to connect with her. To reach out one last time. *I'm sorry, Jordan. I let them trick me. I have to make it right. Please tell Uncle Henry I love him.*

A pulse of energy flashed in the void, and Lilly felt Jordan's scream of despair.

*Look after Owen when he gets better. I love you, Jordan. I'm sorry…*

Lilly closed her watering eyes and concentrated on the Monarch's violent powers battering her mind.

Blood spilled freely from her nose and ears. Her head felt as if it were crumbling apart from the inside. Pain beyond anything she could have even imagined, surged through every part of her.

The swirling lights of the gate throbbed so bright, that it seemed the sun had somehow become trapped down there with them. Now, the great Elders turned their alien minds to her. Powerful thoughts pressed down on her with the strength of an iron clamp, but she channelled her mind to her own light in the void. Forcing aside the Monarch, the Elders, even the spark of her sister's consciousness.

*It will be over soon,* she reassured herself.

Then just like the outside world had been for her entire, short life, her mind fell into silence.

She breathed, and thought once more about Jordan, Uncle Henry, and her brother Owen. Then it was the easiest thing in the world for Lilly to simply reach deep inside herself and turn her light out.

Instantly, the void went black.

ordan's wail of horror mixed with the Monarch's roar of fury as the twisting mass of colours above snapped out of existence. Brody watched, eyes wide with awe as the monstrosity that had been slowly emerging, was sucked back through the whirling colours. A boom of thunder resounded as air raced into the space where the colours had danced just moments ago. High above, Lilly tumbled toward the water.

Turning over and over, he had the horrible image of a discarded doll being tossed aside. Jordan tore down to the lake's edge, launching herself into the inky water.

A moment later, Lilly's body plunged into the lake with a muted splash.

Thrashing her way through the choppy waters, Jordan swam to her sister, arms slashing the water in frenzy.

"We have to help her!" Zoe called, running toward the shore.

Brody turned to the great beast, lying half on the beach, and half in the water, clutching its head as if a sudden pain were ripping at its mind. Spotting the canister in the dirt, he snatched it up and brandished Mike's zippo, still clutched in his other hand. "This ends now!" he yelled.

The Monarch's cold eyes split wide open in alarm. It made a weak, throwaway gesture toward him.

The two smaller creatures charged, slithering at speed. Shaking the canister, he guessed there was about a third of petrol still left. "Be brave! Be brave!" He repeated his mantra.

The creature's words began to press into his mind, but he was ready. *Join us, join us... brave boy!*

Brody sparked the lighter, dropped it in the canister, and hurled it just as his body froze. The creatures wrapped him in their mental trap, and fell upon him.

But the canister hit true, flame catching the petrol. The resulting explosion came with the force of a grenade. The first creature howled as it was engulfed by the flames. The other crashed into him, driving out all the air from his body.

Tearing into his slim frame, slashing the skin of his chest and arms, it roared and hissed with rage.

Bringing down three savage blows, the creature paused to look upon its victim. For a moment, Brody thought he was gazing on the blustering face of Mason from school again.

His nose and cheek cracked under the strikes, and thick, coppery blood seeped down his throat. Through his spinning vision, he saw the other creature slithering this way and that as the flames consumed it.

The one assaulting him abandoned its attack, rushing to drag its kin toward the water but the flames were spreading too fast. The creature's mental hold over him broke as its focus turned to saving the other.

Wiping the blood dripping over his eyes, he spotted Zoe hauling Jordan from the water.

"Jordan, please! You'll never make it out there!" Zoe argued, trying to restrain the much stronger girl.

"No! I'm not leaving her!" Jordan pushed Zoe aside then dived back into the inky blackness of the lake.

The residual light of the gate above was now just a dying glow. The weakened Monarch slid back beneath the surface, its massive, primordial eyes locked on Brody, a voice croaking in his mind, *Brave boy... you think you have won? No, you are going down with us! There is no escaping.*

The remaining creature on the shore abandoned its attempts to save its kin as it flopped and tremored in its death throes. The flames had claimed it. The remaining creature raced with fury toward him, the flames rapidly spreading about the shoreline.

Brody slumped to his knees. The Monarch was right; there was nowhere left to run. At least they had stopped its plans. That was something he could hold on to.

Crouched on the shore, hair matted to her muddy face, tears streaming down her cheeks, Zoe slumped forward in defeat.

The creature slithered to a stop before Brody. Unhurriedly, it reached down and gripped him by the throat, lifting him. Fixing him with those pale, heartless eyes.

As helpless as a newborn, Brody hung there. The bones in his neck began to click out of place, and his already fading vision grew dark.

"Chin up, lad," a gruff voice whispered in his ear. "You're not done yet!"

*Pete!*

Blinding light blazed from behind him. Pete's dry, broken voice reverberated through the cavern. The language a strange and foreign chant. Letting out a squeal of horror, and shielding its eyes against the glare, the creature released him.

"Get out!" Pete's pained voice whispered. "Don't let them take you like they took me!" The light blinked out of existence. "I'm fading, lad… Hurry… get out."

Brody didn't spare a moment. Limping across to Zoe who knelt on the shore, he heaved her to standing.

Together, they looked on the black waters but there was no sign of Jordan. He was about to pull Zoe away, but she shook her arm free. "We can't leave her!"

He glanced back to the creature twisting in the mud, talons rubbing at its blinded eyes. It would recover soon and be on them in a flash. Either way, the lake was their only option, but it sure wasn't a good one.

"Then let's get her out," he said with determination.

Zoe looked down on him with those big green eyes and nodded.

Taking her hand, they dived into the lake.

# 40

Jordan drove herself downward, arms and legs kicking as hard as they could. But Lilly's ghostly frame fell just out of her reach. The child's auburn hair swayed gently, giving the impression of being caught on a breeze.

Blotches of white appeared in Jordan's vision; her need for air was becoming overwhelming, yet she pushed deeper.

A rumble far beneath sent ripples and bubbles shooting up toward her face. She had seen the gargantuan body of the Monarch slip beneath the water as she dove under. It must have hit the bottom and displaced the water of the lake.

Then to her joy, she saw Lilly was caught in one of the ripples and bubbling up toward her. The child looked to be floating through a night sky.

But Jordan's happiness was short lived when she realised that she, too, was being swept up in the ripples. Drifting away from Lilly, she strained against the current.

Closer? No! Just out of reach!

Lilly's body turned, revealing the pale face. Peaceful and serene, like she was only sleeping.

*I must take her back up into the light!*

But her need for air was now so strong, that Jordan couldn't hold her breath any longer. By pure instinct, her mouth opened in search of oxygen. Her throat and lungs were instantly flooded with the thick, oily water.

To her oxygen-deprived brain it felt like a deep breath of crisp air.

At least they would be together down here in the dark. Lilly wouldn't be alone.

Just as the darkness was taking her, the sisters' hands touched. *Together, Lil, we'll be here together–*

Something gripped her wrist.

Jordan was yanked away.

Lilly was instantly lost to the shadows beneath. Another hand around her waist, and she was lurched to the surface. As her head broke the water, she took in the wide eyes of her friends through blotchy vision.

The pair yelled incoherently as they tried to shake her to her senses. She half coughed, half vomited up the horrid water she'd swallowed, took one breath of rancid air, and then faded into unconsciousness.

The vision of Lilly's frail body sinking to the depths below carved into her mind.

# 41

Zoe felt Jordan go limp in her arms. "We lost Lilly!" she yelled. A tear sliding down her cheek was instantly washed away by the rolling waters of the lake. "Just like we lost Mike and Todd." Brody took hold around Jordan's legs, and between them they kept her afloat.

"Look!" Brody said.

She spun to the direction he pointed and saw water falling away under an outcrop of rocks.

"It could be a way out!" he yelled.

"Or it could take us even deeper into these caves!"

A blood-curdling howl of fury from the shoreline caused them both to spin back to the sound. The remaining creature slithered into the shallows, its pale eyes reflecting the crackling flames around the cave which were now spreading up the walls fuelled by the curtain of dried roots.

Diving forward, the creature sped toward them with the pace of a torpedo. Brody paddled desperately toward the outcrop without a word.

Zoe pushed her aching body to swim. The sense of being trapped in one of those nightmares—where no matter how hard you push to go faster, you simply move slower—was suddenly frighteningly real.

The closer to the outcrop they got, the louder the sound of the violent, rushing water. Chancing a look behind her, she saw the creature rocketing toward them.

Wrapping her arm tighter around Jordan's waist, she kicked furiously against the water.

"Just a bit closer!" Brody yelled. The current caught them in a ferocious pull. Rushing water yanked them toward the sinkhole. Zoe's hand found his and she pulled him close, Jordan held afloat between them.

Just then, the creature surged from the water, talons ripping into her back just as they all hit the edge of the sinkhole. Her screams of pain were muffled by the rushing water, and she pulled her friends tightly to her, closed her eyes and held on.

Under they went, bashing about as they were swept deeper and deeper. Surfacing briefly in the pitch black, she took a breath only to be sucked beneath again. Soon, they were bouncing off the slimy rocks as they tumbled through the watery unknown. The creature gave a howl as another steep drop loomed ahead of them. Zoe twisted in the powerful current, and her friends were ripped from her in a second.

Just when she felt she would drown, light blazed above her.

*An escape?*

Suddenly her head broke the surface, she took a desperate breath and opened her eyes. A low hanging rock leered before her and she smacked into it with a nasty, wet thump.

The muffled rumble of the water lingered in her ears a moment longer before everything went silent.

42

The nauseating stench of smoke assaulted him as he regained consciousness. Brody flopped onto his back, eyes blinking open. A cool rush of water flowed beneath him. Above, a pastel orange sky marked the beginnings of sunrise.

Drenched through to the bone, the taste of blood thick in his mouth, he breathed, trying to settle his pounding heart. *I'm alive.*

Black smoked now grew in the air, threatening to block out the glorious morning sun. His mind slowly began to gain some lucidity. Lurching up to an awkward sitting position, he looked gingerly about him. Where were the girls? And where exactly was he?

Rubbing his eyes, he took in the scene around him. A small yet rapidly-flowing waterfall, perhaps three meters high, bubbled and splashed before him. The water rushing out from the jagged mouth of a cave half hidden by the thick growth of the bush. The sinkhole in the lake must have led out here. The smoke stung his eyes. *Don't tell me we've started another bush fire?* he thought with a hint of dark amusement.

Movement in the shallow water beside him sent panic through his body. *The creature!*

But whatever had moved had a matted shock of pink hair crowning its head, spluttering, and coughing. "Jordan? Are you all right?" his voice was little more than a strained whisper over the crashing waters. Her ashen face was mapped with scratches and cuts. "Where's Zoe?" he asked, offering his hand.

"I remember you both had a hold of me, and Lilly was…" Her voice drifted off.

He could see her tears building. "Lilly… She's still in there. I… I couldn't…"

Hugging her tightly, her body shaking with sobs, he felt that sinking feeling drop into his stomach. Had they not gone there to save Lilly? Instead, they had lost her, and Zoe too. The crackling of fire somewhere in the distance now came to his ears. The fire had spread up from the caves again it seemed.

"Zoe!" he yelled; his throat dry as sawdust. "Where are you?"

A deep groan, and shrill scream were his answer. He and Jordan snapped a look of terror at each other.

Zoe appeared, scrambling down the bank of the shallow creek, face white as a sheet. Spotting them, she quickened her pace only to tumble down into the shallows with a splash.

Crimson seeped into the waters, spilling from a nasty slash across her forehead. They struggled to haul her to the shore. Then Jordan stilled, pointing a quivering finger behind them. He spun to look.

Dragging itself toward them was the last creature. Its eyes fell upon him. Its guttural roar of hatred shook the trees. Birds took screeching to the sky and the earth quaked.

The smoke blackened the morning sun, and the crackling of the flames grew louder still. It felt like the four of them, were on some scarlet-painted plain of hell.

The creature was horribly cut and burned. Its movements pained. Yet its intentions clear.

*You will join us, brave boy,* it said into his mind. *You will pay for what you have done!*

The creature hurled itself at him. He braced for the impact as the creature's jaw stretched wide. Talons flexing their razor-sharp tips.

*Thwack!*

Something cannoned into the side of the thing's head. Its body slumped just inches from Brody.

*Smack!*

Something else smashed into the creature. Dazed, it fell forward hissing meekly. He swung around to see the girls, staggering over to him. Their hands held sleek, wet rocks from the shallow creek bed. They hurled a few more at the already battered creature. Crashing flat on its back, barely conscious from the repeated blows to its head, it attempted to rise but slumped again.

Jordan mounted the fallen creature, striking it several times on the side of its bloodied head. Zoe gripped its arm and pinned it to the ground, pressing all her weight down on the broken creature's limb. Jordan did the same.

"Brody!" Jordan yelled, "Grab that and finish it off!" She nodded to a rock about the size of a bowling ball, half submerged in the muddy water.

"Do it!" Zoe screamed.

Hoisting the rock from the mud, Brody lumbered toward them. The creature struggled in vain; too injured to offer much resistance.

This broken thing that twitched and moaned weakly in the growing smoke, and roar of approaching flames, was the last of its kind, he realised.

It lay there. Pale defeated eyes staring up at him. The fight was over.

"What are you waiting for?" Jordan demanded.

Zoe glared up at him with blood shot eyes. "These things killed Lilly. They killed Todd! Finish it!" she screamed. "Now!"

He could end it all right now. So, why did he hesitate? A memory pushed to the front of his mind.

Mason.

The bully from school, standing over him ready to throw down blow, after blow. No! This was different… wasn't it? These things had destroyed his life. They killed his friends. They wanted to wipe out humanity!

So why the hell was he thinking of Mason? Why was he hesitating? Pete's voice echoed through his memory. *It was their place, long before we threw up a fence and called it ours.'*

This thing was just a soldier in a long war. Could he blame it for wanting to take back its home? He tossed the rock aside.

The girls stared in disbelief. Jordan leapt up, snatching the rock up and raising it above her head. "This is for Lilly!"

"Stop!" His hand whipped out catching her arm. He wrestled the rock from her and dropped it aside.

Jordan grabbed him roughly. He raised his hands to calm her.

"Killing it won't bring her back," he said. "I'm truly sorry about Lilly, I am!" he said gently. "But all my life I've seen anger, hate, and violence. Doing this won't make you feel any better."

Zoe was on her feet now, the creature forgotten. "These things are killers, Brody. They'll kill again!"

"They only started attacking all those years ago because we… humans… took this from them," he said, gesturing to the sprawling bushland. "We can stop the cycle here and now without any more killing." Brody looked down at the defeated creature.

Jordan yanked him off the ground. "What if it finds a way to call back those monsters from the other side?"

"It won't," he said.

"How?" she screamed, shaking him so violently he felt he'd rip apart in her grip.

"Because I'm going to stay and… and watch! Just like Pete did!"

The fury in her eyes softened, and she released him. The roar of the flames crackled somewhere close behind them. Jordan's stare was a cocktail of confusion, anger, and sadness.

Gripping her bulging arms, he looked deeply into those hurt eyes. "Please, Jordan. Trust me," he implored.

Pushing him aside, she helped lead Zoe away without looking back.

Zoe did look back, however. Emerald eyes drilling into his soul. He could feel the swirl of emotions burning within as the big greens flittered from him to the creature.

"That fire is getting close," she mumbled. "We should hurry." The pair struggled away into the bush.

The creature and he were left to consider each other. Smoke blackened the morning sun completely. The heat of the fire continued to build around them but still he stood there, and the creature lay wearily gazing up at him, blood dripping down its tree-bark skin.

*I could still kill you now, brave boy.* Its thoughts pressed in on him. He felt the creature mulling that over as it slithered to its towering height. Its hulking shoulders drooped.

Instead of attacking it nodded its great head to the creek, flowing away from the growing fire. *Follow the water.* It slithered away into the bush.

Only when it was gone did he become truly aware of the heat as the flames roared forward. He limped after his friends. Behind him, the fire spread. The hilly bush aflame once more.

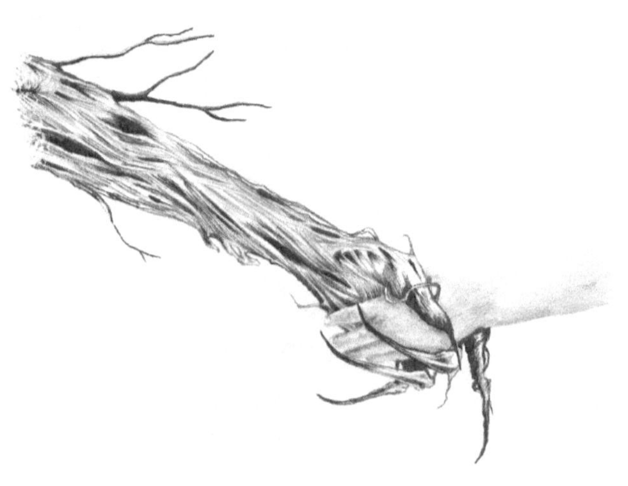

# 43

Jordan kicked at the dirt with a growl of despair as they battled on through the bush. They had been a literal stone's throw from being rid of those things for good. But it wasn't Brody who had convinced Jordan not to kill that thing.

It was Lilly.

Lilly had sacrificed herself to save them. The thought raised a fury within her. Her hands clenched, face bright red with rage. But Brody was right. Killing the last of those monsters wouldn't bring her beautiful sister back. Casting a glance at Brody through bloodshot and swollen eyes, she felt the anger drain as her fists relaxed.

*He better do as he promised.*

Tears fell, but she trudged on. Eventually, they came to one of the highways that led into the estate. Clambering over the metal guardrail, she looked back to see the orange glow of the flames and billowing black smoke filling the morning sky.

The flashing lights of fire trucks were visible at the bush line. They'd gotten there fast but she recalled that some police had been on the boundary fence already.

"They can't know we were out there," said Zoe. "They'll never believe the truth. And the fact that Saunders was out there too…" she trailed off.

They struggled down the road toward the estate. Zoe was right; if the authorities found out they'd been out in the bush, they would have an impossible time explaining the death of a detective.

Passing the homes on the outskirts of the estate, Jordan caught a glimpse of the trio in the reflection of a curtained window.

With clothes torn, faces bruised and bloodied, they clearly stood out against the fresh cut lawns and earth-coloured houses.

Jordan steered them toward a walkway between two large homes where they slumped to the cool concrete. "We should split up and get home," she muttered flatly. "Before everyone comes out to see the action."

Brody reached out. "Jordan… I… I'm so sorry about Lilly—"

"We need to get going," she cut in. Without another word, the three dragged themselves off the concrete, and made for the street. The others hurried away, giving her a quick hug before they went.

Once they were gone, Jordan slipped to her knees in the middle of the street. Vision flooding with tears as reality slammed home.

She would never see Lilly again.

Never.

Even the drone of an approaching car couldn't bring her to move. The devastation, the loss, it had broken her last strains of fortitude. The car's brakes screeched. Jordan limped to standing and tried to step off the road before this stranger came to investigate but then a familiar voice called.

"Jordy?" Beneath flowing, grey locks and drooping brows were the bright eyes she knew so well.

"Uncle Henry?" she whispered through her tears.

He was out of the car and charging toward her, arms wide. She collapsed into them. He squeezed her so tight, that for a moment she couldn't even breathe.

"I've been looking for you all night!" he said, his voice strained with breaking emotion. "Where the bloody hell were you?"

"I… I was looking for Lilly," she stated, her voice broken. He frowned, "Jordan? What happened?"

For the first time in many years, Jordan's walls of stoicism crumbled. She gripped on to him, not wanting to ever let go for fear of losing him too.

## 44

Leading Zoe from the police station, her dad forced a smile as he opened the car door guiding her inside. Three days since the fire, and police had been questioning her and Brody nonstop.

What did they know? Where did those cuts and bruises come from? Where were they when the fire started? Who could prove that?

The one thing they'd pressed them hardest on was the whereabouts of Detective Saunders. He'd taken a very keen interest in them since they'd returned. Had he been in contact since he came to question her the night of the fire?

It went on for hours every day.

But Zoe knew the drill. All the evidence was circumstantial. The police had nothing solid, and both had managed to make it home and clean up before their parents had woken up. The cuts had been from a night of drinking at the skate park, they'd said. The cops hadn't bought that for a second; however, there was no solid proof to discount their story.

Finally, the police had released them. But they were subjected to some fearsome glares from the officers as they'd left the station.

Her father steered the car out of the parking lot and onto the main road. Reaching for his chubby arm, she offered him her classic private school smile, "Dad?"

"Yes, Zoe?" he said, in a voice of distant formality that suggested he was angry but also weary.

"We really didn't do anything, I promise."

He tensed, subtly moving his arm away. "Both you and I know that's a lie."

"But Dad… you don't understand—"

"Enough," he said defeated. "I'm sure you'll tell me the truth one day."

Folding her hands in her lap, she kept quiet for the rest of the drive.

Her eyes almost popped out of her head as she pushed through the front door to see her mother standing there with phone in hand. She gave Zoe a quick hug and peck on the cheek, flicking her wavy blonde locks from her face, and offering a sympathetic smile.

"Sweetheart! Thank goodness you're back. Now, do we need to get you the lawyer we spoke about?" She cupped Zoe's face in her hands. "You all good, love?"

She nodded. "They think it was Brody and I who lit the fire—"

Her mother's phone burst into life, and she held up a hand to silence her daughter. "Hello? Yes? Sure, I'm not busy. I needed to call you about that contract anyway."

Giving Zoe another peck on the cheek and mouthing the words, *We'll talk later,* she headed to her office, shutting the door behind her.

It was like she'd caught a glimpse of some rare bird that everyone believed was extinct. Her father plodded up the stairs to his own office, and she was left awkwardly standing in the walkway near the front door.

Looking about the lush home with all its comforts, she wiped a single tear. This place had never felt like home. Opening the front door, she slipped out.

With the familiar mountain breeze whipping around her, she dwelled on what a lonely place Golden Pastures was. And she didn't want to be alone right now.

After walking for a time, she turned on to the road leading to the empty plots. Arriving at Jordan's house, she saw that Lilly's crayon drawings covering the sloping driveway had faded to dull, lifeless smudges.

"Can I help you?" She spun to the gruff voice. Jordan's uncle was leaning on the front door frame. He held a mug of tea, the vapours drifting up and fading in the sunshine.

Swallowing nervously, she plastered on her polite, private school smile again. "Hello, Mr Jenkins. I was just wanting to catch up with

Jordan if she was around?"

He flicked his tea on to the lawn calling into the house as he did. "Jordy!" Calmly, he strode across the lawn toward her. "Zoe? Isn't it? Jordy told me about your little expedition," he said, bending low to eye her. "I don't know what sort of games you and that little freak play, but you keep her out of them."

He cracked his neck as he spoke but after what she'd survived, this old man just wasn't really intimidating. Still, she knew to at least give the air of being diplomatic and hastily nodded her acquiescence.

Straightening, he walked into the house as Jordan appeared in the doorway. Flashing a weary smile at Zoe, she saw her face was mapped with the scars of their escape, and for the first time, Zoe saw a deep vulnerability in her friend's eyes.

Her uncle disappeared inside. Yet, Zoe felt his gaze fixed on her from behind the curtain of the living room window.

Jordan pulled her into a tight embrace. "Jesus, I'm glad to see you, rich girl."

Zoe pressed her face into the pink haired beast's shoulder. "You ok…" she started to ask but broke off with a shake of her head. "Sorry, that's a really stupid question."

"We're ok," Jordan said flatly. "The police are out searching again but they're being careful to keep the media out of it. Last thing I need is cameras and whatever all over the street. Uncle Henry knows. But he doesn't believe me. Thinks its trauma making me talk crazy."

Zoe nodded her understanding. "Jordan," she said as they broke their hug. "I really thought that this time we could save—"

Jordan shook her head. "Lilly saved *us*. She saved everyone. You saw that thing that was coming through the gate." She scratched her foot across the grass, a weary sigh escaping her throat. "It's done now. But it makes my skin crawl to know that thing is still out there."

Zoe nodded her understanding. "Brody promises he'll keep watch and I believe him."

Jordan flicked her fringe out of her eyes. The wind lashed the street from the fence line. "Are you going to stay too?" she asked hopefully.

Zoe shook her head. "I have to go back to school. In a way, I'm glad I'll be out of that house, away from this fucking place," she said with a nod to the empty plots.

Jordan offered a sly smile. "I thought you didn't swear?"

"Fuck that!" said Zoe. "Last thing I'm worried about anymore." She took Jordan's hand. "Listen, two years ago, Brody and I promised we'd stay in contact but we didn't." She gave Jordan's hand a squeeze. "I don't want to make that mistake again."

Jordan gave a nod of understanding, and Zoe embraced her. She spotted the weathered face of Jordan's uncle glaring out at her from behind the curtain now.

"I better get going," Zoe said kindly. "My folks are pretty dark on me at the moment."

Jordan flashed a smile. "I can imagine. Call me later, ok?"

"I will."

"And rich girl?" Jordan shuffled nervously. "I'm going back out there."

"What?" Zoe hissed in shock. "Why?"

"To get Lilly's body. To get Lilly out of there," she said. "She deserves to be in the light. Not down there."

"But Jordan—"

"You can't stop me." It wasn't a threat, just a statement of fact.

"Then I'll come with you," she replied in the same matter of fact voice.

Jordan smiled thankfully and headed inside.

After giving the old boundary fence and the empty plots a glare, Zoe moved off. Her phone buzzed. A message from Brody appeared. 'Meet at Pete's. Sundown. Important!'

Zoe looked up to the front door. Jordan had her phone out too. The pair shared a knowing nod as her uncle ushered her inside.

Whatever Brody was planning, she prayed it didn't involve their one remaining friend left in the bush.

# 45

itting on the porch steps, knees hugged to his chin, Brody drank in the surrounding blackened bush.

Running his hand over the rough boards of the house's veranda, a gentle pulsing energy in the wood caused the little hairs on his knuckles to stand up. Shutting his eyes, he welcomed the energy to flow through him. Giggled at the strange sensation.

*There is more to this world. Pete knew it, Lilly knew it, and now it seems it's revealing itself to me.*

Opening his eyes, he took in the setting sun. Listened to the cries of the many birds as they welcomed the night. The sky was turning a deep crimson, and the crickets took up the song of twilight.

Would the girls show?

After a while, twilight began its slow descent into night, and Brody sensed them before he heard them. Their energies wafted to him through some sort of mental void in the recesses of his mind.

Pushing through the scrub, their weary eyes told the story of the last few weeks. They were broken and beaten. Yet they were still here… Well, not all of them.

Now, he felt something approaching from the bush. The connection between him and the land was growing.

Something was awakening within him, pulling him toward the natural world; and yet it only seemed strong when he was here, near Pete's house.

"Brody?" Jordan's agitated voice brought him back.

"Sorry what?" he said.

"I asked if you're all right?"

"Yeah," he said with a half-smile.

"How is this house still standing?" she asked with wonder.

He grinned. "I think there is still a shred of old Pete in there protecting his sanctuary."

Zoe held her hands out with a shrug. "Well? We're here. What's this all about? Why are we out in this fucking place again?"

"You're swearing is getting out of control, Zo," he said with a chuckle.

She shook her head in frustration. "Just tell us what you want."

Night was casting its blanket across their little patch of the earth. A crunch of leaves and a rustle of the bushes told of the arrival of his other guest. The girls' heads snapped between him and the noise.

"Don't be afraid." He clutched his hands to his chest. "Just trust me," he pleaded.

Zoe was aghast. "You don't mean… Brody, you can't be serious!"

The sound of something being dragged across the ash and rocks grew from the gathering night. Their eyes cast to the other side of the clearing. Zoe stepped behind Jordan, hitting Brody with a glare that screamed betrayal.

"It's ok," he offered calmingly.

The creature's hulking outline took shape in the blackness. It inched toward the clearing as if expecting a trap. He spotted a small, dark object balancing on the back of its tail.

Passing through the burnt trees, it stretched to tower above them. Still looking the primal terror it had always been. The creature's hateful eyes fell upon them, but he sensed its pain, and above all, he sensed its melancholy.

Jordan dropped into her fight stance but Brody stepped between them, just as the creature curled its body to strike.

"Wait!" he said firmly.

She retreated. Zoe wrapped her arms around her friend in solace. "What is that fucking thing doing here," she screamed at him.

The creature hissed back, still deadly despite its weakened state.

"I asked it to come," he continued gently. "Just as I asked you two here." He breathed, gathering his thoughts. "Zoe, remember when the disappearances first started? You discovered there was a pattern. Every fourteen years people just seemed to wander into the bush. That was the cycle for them to grow their young. They were always planning on rising again. To try and take back this world from us and…" He looked to the creature. "…they almost achieved it. But humanity moves too quick for them. We spread too fast."

Jordan's furious eyes held him. "Last time I looked, Brody, *you* were human! Are you siding with this thing? It killed your friends! Killed Lilly! She died saving us from these monsters. I can't believe I listened to you. I should have ended it when I had the chance!"

The creature let out a shrill roar, the sound causing them all to clutch at their ears. Then he heard it speak in his head. He looked to the others; they'd heard it too!

It slithered forward, bent low, and it was all he could do to not sprint for the boundary fence and home.

*I am…* Its words faltered in his mind, but it drew itself up again. *I am the last.*

Its misery was palpable, and he felt that on some level Jordan was empathetic. After all, she had lost all her close family, as had this creature.

Brody spoke up. "That's why I wanted to offer a truce. I think that's what it's called," he said. His voice was unsure, but he hoped he was covering it with enough false confidence. "We leave it alone," he said, gesturing to the creature. "And *you* leave *us* alone."

*One thing I am now…is alone,* it rumbled in their minds.

Zoe suddenly stepped toward him but kept her eyes firmly on the creature. "How can you trust it?" she spat angrily.

*How can I trust you?* the creature retorted.

Brody raised his hands; a placating gesture. "Because I'm going to stay and watch. Not just to keep an eye on it," he said. "But to keep an eye on us too." He pointed up the hill to the estate. "I know you will begin to build up your numbers again," he said to the creature. "You must use the animals, not humans. Otherwise, they *will* come looking eventually. I will make sure to keep them away, and keep you hidden."

The creature's pale eyes took him in. *You truly are a brave boy, aren't you? I could kill all three of you right here.*

"You need me," Brody pushed. "I have …the power growing within me. Just like Pete did." He nodded to the house.

The creature's mouth twisted in what must be a smile. *You've spent too much time in the caves with us, brave boy.*

Brody ignored it. "Do we have a deal?"

A grunt was its response. Then reaching behind it, the thing took the object balancing on its tail. Gently it lifted it, slithered toward Jordan, and lay it before her. Brody saw that it was a bundle of leaves and mud. But he knew what the earthy coating preserved.

Jordan frowned from the creature to Brody. He offered a sad smile, and saw the realisation fall on her. Jordan dashed forward ripping the leaves and mud away. The ashen face of Lilly was revealed, the little girl's expression tranquil. Strands of hair fluttered in the bush's evening winds.

"I'm going to take you back to the light, Lil," Jordan whispered, cradling the child, and stroking her cheek. "You're with Mum and Dad now, aren't you?"

Without looking back, Jordan lifted Lilly's frail frame and moved toward the path heading back to the estate.

Zoe followed. "I hope you're right about this," she said to Brody.

Now it was only him and the creature. It flicked its tail and turned toward the bush, but Brody stepped after it. *And what of the Monarch? And the… what do you call them? Elders? The things from beyond the gate.*

The creature did not turn. *The Elders are still there in the void. But without our great numbers, and the Monarch, they are unreachable.*

Brody nodded. *Did the Monarch survive?*

Now it turned. *The Monarch always survives. But now he slumbers deep beneath these hills. His power is drained. It will be many cycles before he wakes again.*

*How do I know you won't try and wake him?* Brody asked, a hint of threat in his thoughts.

The creature turned away. *The same way I know you will not come to kill me or my new young. Trust.*

*So, we have a deal?*

The creature slithered away toward the darkness of the bush.

*I asked if we have a deal?* He sent the thought toward his former foe.

It flicked its tail but did not look back at him. *Yes,* it replied simply, slipping away into the night.

Brody collapsed to his knees, tears of relief and exhaustion falling. It was finally over.

46

Lilly's funeral was an intimate affair. Laid to rest beneath a gum tree in the large cemetery just off the highway, Jordan had made sure the spot got plenty of sun. Zoe and Brody chose to keep a respectful distance. It was a family affair after all, and Jordan's uncle was barely tolerating their presence as it was.

Apart from Jordan's uncle, a few of his friends and a dark-haired, sickly-looking man—which Brody insisted must be Jordan's brother, Owen—the service was small.

Jordan had said she'd told the authorities that she'd gone searching for Lilly and made the grim discovery in one of the water holes deep in the bush.

The police were not at all convinced.

But again, there was no evidence to disprove what Jordan said. They had told the media their investigations were ongoing and asked them to respect the family's privacy.

As the funeral ended, Jordan embraced the sickly man, who was then led to a car by two others in hospital orderly attire before being driven away.

Jordan watched the car forlornly, her black dress billowing in the familiar afternoon mountain winds. Her uncle ushered her away and just like that, the service was over.

Together, Zoe and Brody headed to the bus stop. "You all right?" she asked him, breaking their contemplative silence.

His weary eyes peering up at her from beneath that brown mop of hair was her only answer.

"Yeah," she said, taking his hand. "Me too."

183

A few days later, Zoe lay on her bed in the glow of the afternoon sun streaming through her window, half awake and lolling in and out of disconnected dreams. A buzz of her phone startled her fully awake.

Snatching it up, Jordan's name was revealed. Opening it, she read the message. It took a few reads for it to really sink in.

'Thanks for being there, rich girl. I will see you again. But I need to be alone for a while.'

What the hell did that mean?

Shaking herself awake properly, she was about to reply, but she had the feeling that she must get to her friend and speak to her face to face.

Pulling on her shoes, she stumbled downstairs and out the front door in seconds.

Sprinting around to Jordan's street, a growing dread descended on her. She pushed herself to run faster. What was Jordan going to do?

Coming to a halt at the top of the street, hands on knees, she took deep, settling breaths. The sense that she may already be too late was growing by the moment.

Looking toward Jordan's house, she stepped back when she saw a pair of uniformed police standing on the lawn with Jordan's uncle. All three men stared at her. Their eyes spoke of their loathing. Approaching cautiously, she strained to hear the conversation.

The police made a show of turning their backs as she approached. "Don't worry, Mr Jenkins, she can't have gone far. She's probably just upset and went for a walk or something. We'll find her," one of the officers said. They shook the elder man's hand and hurried to their squad car.

Jordan's uncle immediately walked back to the front door. Zoe ran toward him, calling in breathless gasps. "Wait! Jordan sent me a text and—"

Lurching around, he stalked toward her with menacing strides. "I don't know what the hell you dragged her into, but Lilly is dead!" Tears built in his eyes.

Seeing the commotion, the police scrambled back out of their car.

His hands gripped her roughly by the arms. "And Jordy is gone," he growled. "Whatever you and that little bastard got yourselves involved with, you just keep it away from me! Or I swear—"

"Mr Jenkins, calm down!" one of the police said soothingly as he pulled the old man's hands off Zoe.

The other officer shoved her toward the street. "We've all heard enough out of you!" he pushed her again, this time with real force.

"Lilly saved us, Mr Jenkins, all of us!" she cried.

The policeman made a move toward her, but she dashed back up the street.

All night, Zoe attempted to reach Jordan but her calls went straight to message bank.

Eventually, she tossed the phone aside, flopped on her bed and wept.

Was it her fault that Lilly had been taken? But how could they've known she would go into the bush? Why had she gone there when Zoe had warned her?

*Because she was a lonely little girl, and those things tricked her... and there is still one more out there.*

If Brody were wrong, she would never forgive him for letting it live. A gentle knock on her door sounded and she wiped her tears. This would be her dad coming to do his fatherly duty, she supposed. She tried to plaster her fake smile across her tear-stained face, but it didn't feel very convincing this time.

A ripple of shock passed through her when her mother's head poked around the door. "Zoe?" she asked. "Are you ok?"

It had been so long since she talked to her mother that the woman's voice still sounded strange. Yet her concern seemed genuine; Zoe could see it in her face.

She hung her head. "No, Mum. I'm not."

The wind bit at Brody as he rode toward home, bringing him back into the moment. Winter had arrived, and it was going to be a long and nasty one.

He was desperate to see his mum again. Desperate to be away from Golden Pastures and all the pain the place had wrought on him and his friends.

It would be easy enough to leave, and if he was honest with himself, he'd almost been ready to do just that. Then he would think of Lilly's sacrifice. He'd felt that horrible moment when she departed this world. The flame of her presence in the mental void he was growing more aware of, had been extinguished by Lilly's own hand. The child's mind was the gate, and she had slammed it closed to save not just them, but the whole world from the horrors beyond.

It cut him deeply to think of that bright little spark gone well before her time. How he wished he'd gotten to know the kid; to try and understand her and what she might have been capable of. He had a strong feeling that whatever the ability was that she possessed, was related to what was developing within him now.

He rubbed at his temples. The entire series of events had been a whirlwind, which had sucked them up and spat them out the other side. All these months later and he still mused on it all, mused on Lilly every day.

Swinging his bike into the driveway of the Giant's house, he hopped off Rusty and parked it in its spot by the fence. His dad's truck wasn't in the drive, which meant the Giant was still at work.

Perfect.

Dumping his school bag inside, he locked the front door and walked through the tangle of streets, toward the empty plots.

Once there, he stole around the edge of the fence to avoid possibly running into Jordan's uncle. Slipping through the opening in the fence, he descended the overgrown path toward the ancient house.

His awareness of the life in the bush grew the closer he got. It was almost like he could feel the land breathing, sense the animals and other… thing… within the bush.

*You are waking up to the life of the land,* a familiar presence said in his mind. His slim body tensed as he stepped into the clearing, and saw the creature hunched in front of the crumbling house.

Keeping a respectful distance, he stood as confidently as he could. At least he hoped he was convincing.

*Greetings, brave boy,* it said in his head.

Brody swallowed his nerves. *Have you started to… ah…* What was the word he was looking for? *…grow… your new young?*

The thing sniffed. *Yes, I used the tree dweller. It was old anyway.*

Brody frowned; tree dweller? He pondered for a second. *Do you mean a Koala?'*

The thing whipped its tail and scratched at the dirt. *If that's what you two-legs name those fat, furry things, then yes.*

He nodded; the truce was keeping… so far.

*And what of you, brave boy? You said you would keep my home safe.*

*I have!* Brody replied. *I've set up an environmental recommendation, to keep this entire area of land free from development. The local council backed it and everything and…*

This time the creature's sniff had a touch of confusion behind it. He guessed that local government procedures, and environmental activism was probably lost on the thing.

*Trust me, you won't be seeing any two-legs around here if I can help it. Well, apart from me, of course.*

Sliding to its full height, it stretched its arms. *I must return to the young,* it stated in Brody's mind. Then it suddenly bent low. Its face just inches from his, those pale eyes holding him in place. Hot acrid breath assaulted his nostrils. *Would you like to… join us?*

The energies pushed at his mind. His body twitched and for a split second he thought the creature had gained control over him. Heart racing, a horrible panic pounded at his gut. The energies twisted and whipped through him. But it passed. It seemed the creature could no longer wield its control. It gave a curious nod, turned and slid calmly off into the growing night.

*Until our next meeting, brave boy.*

The peace, truce, or deal—whatever he wanted to call it—would hold… Brody hoped.

His gaze drifted to the archaic house. It held no fear for him now. Moving toward the splintered door, his footsteps creaking across the rotting boards, he shouldered the door open, breathing in musty air. Despite the cobweb-coated windows, and howl of wind through the many cracks in the walls, he sensed a deep power pulsing with life. It felt familiar. It felt like Pete.

He had a lot to learn about this new responsibility he'd taken on. In fact, it was more than that; it was a new life. And this house had things to teach him.

"You're still here, aren't you, Pete?"

He moved through to the table where once he, Zoe and Mike had sat with Pete on a moonlit night.

Brody dusted the rickety chair with his hand and sat, closing his eyes. He slumped down, calm, and relaxed.

This place felt like a sanctuary, it felt like home.

# 48

Deep into the caves it slid. The phosphorus light was not as prevalent this deep, but the creature didn't need to see down here. It had discovered an area deeper than the great lake, deeper than any two-legs would ever go. At least not on their own accord.

Dropping through a slim opening in the wet rock, it came to rest in the dark. Listened.

Something gave a moan of pain; something very human. The creature reached out and stroked the head of a boy two-leg. The boy screamed, his voice's echo bounced back at him, mocking his cries of terror.

The creature ran its talons over the boy's grossly, swollen belly. It was impressed at the young human's longevity.

It had found it happily astride one of those strange, two-wheeled contraptions like the ones the brave boy and his friends had travelled around on. He'd been with some other young two-legs near one of the fences behind the human dwellings, doing some form of writing on the fence with strange hissing cans while sucking on little fire sticks and blowing smoke out their mouths. Two-legs really did have strange habits. Once the boy had left his friends, taking him had been as easy as plucking newborn birds from their nest.

While the brave boy's mind was growing stronger, the rest of the two-legs were still the mentally dim animals they'd always been.

Yes, the brave boy was becoming like the old man, and that could be a problem in the future, but the creature had something the brave boy didn't.

Time.

It intended to regrow the young, swelling their numbers to even greater than before. And when the time came, the creature would lead them to the surface and take back the world of men. It only hoped the brave boy would still be alive to see it. For humans grew old and withered much faster than they.

Oh, how it yearned for the boy to see. Wanted him to regret the mercy he'd shown. For the creature would show none when the time came. *The closing of the gate may have defeated the Monarch, and closed off the way for the Elders, but I am here. I am alive,* it thought with a satisfied growl.

It ripped a talon across its captive's stomach. Dozens of grey slugs burst forth, squirming to the floor. The young were born!

The boy screamed.

The creature smiled.

# Until the Storm Passes by Stefan Taylor

*On a summer night, in a forgotten town, a storm is brewing…*

It was supposed to be a quick stop for a bite to eat, on their journey to a new life. But when Sisters Jordan, Lilly and their older brother Owen, arrive in the town of Barnsford, they soon find themselves at the mercy of malevolent forces beyond their understanding.

Trapped in the town by a fierce storm, and with nowhere to run, the siblings are not just fighting for their lives; they are fighting for their souls as well!

*www.stefantaylorauthor.com*

## *Sick Little Pupplies by Stefan Taylor and Simon J Green*

*A collection of short horror stories you can rip through in hours, but will haunt you for days.*

Demons that draw on a family's misery. The violent deaths of clients from hell. Serial killers and cursed cures that don't turn out how you'd expect. Stefan Taylor builds dark worlds full of classic tension and fear. Simon J Green weaves visually rich tales of carnage and humour. Together, they bring you previously published work alongside original stories designed to scare, shock, and make you feel sick.

*www.stefantaylorauthor.com*

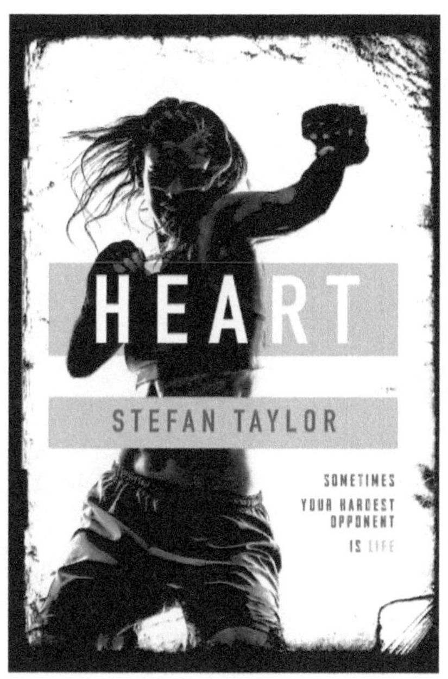

## *Heart by Stefan Taylor*

*The world is their battleground, and life is their opponent.*

When Rose is arrested for assaulting a girl at her high school, the eighteen year old is given one last chance to turn her life around. Sentenced to community service at a local boxing gym, she meets Cathy, a rough, old school trainer, who reluctantly takes the wayward teen under her wing.

For Ila, it seems everyday she deals with her brother's troubles with the law, her father's depression and her mother's constant pressure to succeed in her studies. But she has one escape from the struggles of living up to her immigrant parent's expectations, martial arts. It is her passion and her path.

The two are about to embark on a journey that will ultimately bring them together and entwine their lives.

*www.stefantaylorauthor.com*